FOOD FITNESS AND HEALTH

PART ONE – YOU AND YOUR FOOD

Judy Tatchell and Dilys Wells
Designed by Nerissa Davies

CONTENTS

Illustrated by Sue Stitt, Brenda Haw, Kuo Kang Chen, Martin Newton, Stuart Trotter, Patti Pearce, Ian Jackson, Adam Willis, Sue Walliker, Chris Lyon, John Shackell and Roger Stewart.

Why do you need food?

The first part of this book is all about food. It tells you why you need food, which sorts of food are good for you, which are not so good and why.

Your whole body is made from the food you eat and all your energy comes from food. Without food, you would not be able to move around, keep warm or get better when you injure yourself. Below, you can find out about the different substances in food which you need in order to stay healthy.

Nutrients

Food is made up of lots of different things. Those which your body needs in order to work properly, grow and repair itself, are called nutrients.

Nutrients have different jobs, though many also work together or need the presence of others to work properly. The different types of nutrient are described on these two pages. You can find out more about all of them on the following pages.

Carbohydrate

Carbohydrate gives you energy. Bread and cereal contain a lot of carbohydrate.

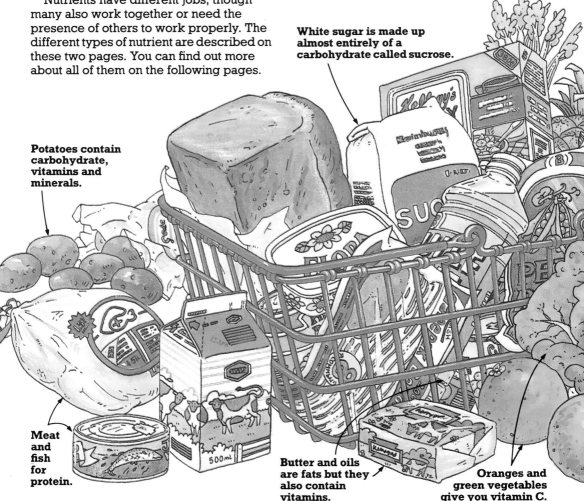

White sugar is made up almost entirely of a carbohydrate called sucrose.

Potatoes contain carbohydrate, vitamins and minerals.

Meat and fish for protein.

Butter and oils are fats but they also contain vitamins.

Oranges and green vegetables give you vitamin C.

Protein

Protein is used to build your body. Almost 20% of your weight is protein. Meat, fish and milk are good sources of protein.

Fat

Your body can store fat and use it later for energy. Meat fat, butter and oils are almost pure fat.

How do you get energy from food?

Your food comes either from animals, e.g. meat and milk, or from plants, e.g. potatoes and peas. When you have eaten and digested the food, your body can use the energy stored by the animal or plant.

Milk

Peas

Meat

Fries

Plants have to make their own food. They get the energy to do this from the sun.

When a cow eats grass, it uses the nutrients made by the grass. So the energy and nutrients you get from food such as beef and milk come first of all from plants.

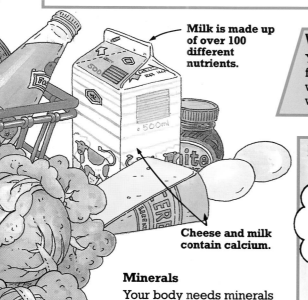

Milk is made up of over 100 different nutrients.

Cheese and milk contain calcium.

Water

You can live for several weeks without food but you will die within a few days without water. Your body is about 66% water.

Minerals

Your body needs minerals such as calcium (to help make bones and teeth) and iron (for your blood). You only need minerals in tiny quantities, though.

Vitamins

You need small amounts of about 20 nutrients called vitamins. These do different things. Vitamin C, for instance, helps glue body cells together to make firm muscles and smooth skin.

Body repair

Most of the dust in your bedroom is your own dead skin cells.

Your body is made up of microscopic building blocks called cells. An adult human body has about fifty million million cells. Throughout your life cells die and are replaced with new ones, using nutrients (mainly protein) from your food. You can see this happening as a suntan fades. Tanned skin is worn away and replaced by new, lighter layers of skin underneath.

3

Growth and repair food

Until you are about 18, your body makes new cells in order to grow. Also, throughout your life, cells wear out and are replaced. Some types of cell only last a few weeks. Others last much longer. After seven years, each cell in an adult's body (except tooth and brain cells) has died and been replaced. All the material for new cells comes from food. Protein is the main body-building nutrient-but you also need others such as vitamins and minerals. A shortage of any nutrient will weaken you and slow down growth and the rate at which you replace worn out cells.

What are proteins made of?

Proteins are made up of substances called amino acids. There are 20 types of amino acid which combine in different ways to make different proteins.

Proteins made up of different combinations of amino acids.

Amino acids combining to make different proteins.

Amino acid

Inside your digestive system*, proteins are broken down into amino acids. They can then be used to build different proteins for body tissues such as muscle, hair, skin and blood cells.

You get protein from foods which come from animals, such as meat and milk, and from plants, such as cereals, beans and nuts. A mother's milk has the very best protein. It has to provide everything a baby needs. A vegan** (someone who does not eat meat or animal products) needs a wide variety of plant proteins to provide all the necessary amino acids.

Protein per 100g of food

Roast beef	25g	(0.9 oz)
Roast chicken	25g	(0.9 oz)
Hard cheese	25g	(0.9 oz)
Grilled cod	20g	(0.9 oz)
Eggs	12g	(0.7 oz)
Milk	3g	(0.1 oz)
Peanuts	28g	(1.0 oz)
Wholemeal bread	10g	(0.4 oz)
White bread	8g	(0.3 oz)
Baked beans	5g	(0.2 oz)
Boiled peas	5g	(0.2 oz)

Protein foods

Most food, except sugar and fat, contains some protein. Meat, fish, nuts and cheese are richest in protein. Much of your protein probably comes from foods such as bread which is only about 10% protein but which you may eat in large quantities.

A 12 year old needs about 55g (2oz) of protein a day. Here are some foods with the amount of protein in them per 100g (3.5oz).

*More about your digestive system on pages 32-33.
**More about vegans on pages 34-35.

Body building

Vitamin C helps cement your body cells together.

The way your body uses protein is similar to the way in which a builder uses bricks to build a house.

The builder cannot work unless he has enough bricks. You cannot grow unless you have enough protein.

He needs a steady supply of concrete and cement as well as bricks. Your body needs regular vitamins and minerals as well as protein.

Food for growth

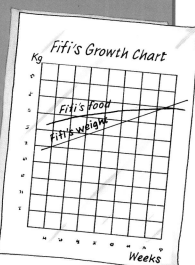

Three slices of lean meat, 28g (1oz) of cheese, two slices of wholemeal bread and a large glass of milk give you enough protein for a day.

Keep your own growth chart

You may grow more quickly in the summer. Sunshine lets you make vitamin D which you need to build bones. Measure your height every month and record the readings. See if your chart shows different growth rates during the year.

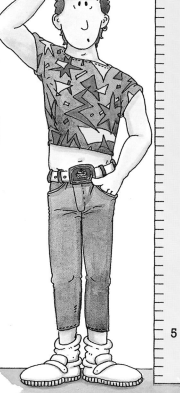

Most children reach half their final adult height by their second birthday, but you grow fastest in your mid-teens. A ten year old boy usually needs at least as much food as his mother. By the age of 12 he is likely to be eating a lot more than his mother as his growth speeds up. Most girls do not grow as tall as most boys so they need slightly less food.

Measuring a pet's growth

If you have a young pet, you can compare how much it eats with how much it grows. Weigh the food you give it each day. Keep a record of your pet's age, weight and the amount of food it eats each week. Try drawing a graph to make a comparison.

How to weigh your pet:
1. Weigh yourself.
2. Weigh yourself holding pet.
3. Subtract (1) from (2).

Fifi's Growth Chart

Kg

Fifi's food

Fifi's weight

Weeks

5

Energy food

You probably need more energy between the ages of 12 and 17 than at any other time in your life, because growing uses a lot of energy. Without energy you would be like a car with no petrol.

Almost all food, except salt and water, gives you some energy. The main sources are carbohydrate and fat, but you can also get energy from protein. The charts on pages 44-45 show what foods are good for energy.

Where does energy come from?

The sun's energy gets locked into plants by a process called photosynthesis during which they make their food. The word means "building up by means of light". Plants make simple sugars using water, light, gases in the air and minerals from the soil.

Water and minerals absorbed through roots.

When you eat an apple you can taste the sugar.

All the energy you get from food starts with the sugars made by plants. Plants use these sugars to build more complex nutrients such as proteins.

A potato stores starch to make new plants next season.

Some plants store energy for later use by combining sugars to make starch. When you eat the plant you can use the stored energy yourself. Sugar and starch are carbohydrates.

Measuring energy

Energy you get from food is measured in calories. These are the same as kilocalories (Kcal) which are used to measure heat energy in physics. Different foods provide you with different amounts of energy.

Here, you can see roughly how many calories certain foods and drinks contain and some examples of what you can do with the energy they give you.

300 calories

Bar of chocolate

Sit a three hour exam.

Swim round a pool for 45 minutes without touching the sides.

75 calories

Slice of buttered toast

Cycle for ten minutes.

Sleep for one and a half hours.

How many calories do you need?

Some people need more calories than others, depending on how big and active they are and how efficiently their bodies use food. Between the ages of ten and 14 you probably need between 2,000 and 3,000 calories a day.

50 calories

Apple

Jog for four minutes.

Scrub the floor for five minutes.

100 calories

Glass of milk

Dance for ten minutes.

Watch TV for one and a quarter hours.

15 calories

Cup of tea

Play football for two minutes.

Walk the dog for three minutes.

How do you use your calories?

About half your calories are used for physical energy and about half for growth, breathing, digestion and so on. The more active you are, the more calories you use, though even when you are asleep your body is using energy.

Using energy foods

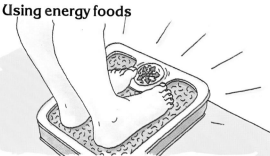

If you eat more carbohydrate and fat than you need for energy, or more protein than you need for growth and repair, your body stores them as fat.

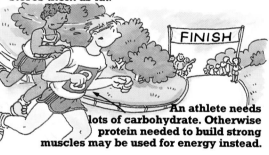

An athlete needs lots of carbohydrate. Otherwise protein needed to build strong muscles may be used for energy instead.

If you do not eat enough food to supply you with the energy you need, your body uses protein for energy instead of for growth and repair.

Vitamin spark plugs

You need certain vitamins to enable your body to release energy from the food you eat. This is similar to a car which needs a spark plug to ignite its petrol. There is more about vitamins on pages 10-11.

Starvation

If people do not get enough to eat, for instance during a famine, any food they do eat is used for energy to stay alive. This is why starving children do not grow. If they do not get enough energy from food, they start using protein from their flesh and muscles, so they waste away.

Energy stores

Your body stores energy for later use in the form of fat. Fat is a very concentrated source of energy. Weight for weight, it provides twice as much energy as carbohydrate or protein. However, too much fat is bad for you, as shown on these pages, so it is better to eat carbohydrate for energy.

Fat for survival

Fat makes up between 20% and 30% of a young woman's body weight and between 10% and 15% of a young man's.

Females have more fat on their bodies than males. This may be nature's way of making sure that in times of food shortage enough women survive to have children.

Do you need fat?

Carrying around extra fat means your heart has to work harder.

You need some body fat to cushion your internal organs, protect your bones and provide an insulating layer round you like a thin blanket. If you eat too much fat, this blanket becomes like an over-stuffed duvet.

Fats are made from substances called fatty acids. Some of these are needed for growth, healthy skin and resistance to infection. Vitamins A and D occur only in certain fats, but your body can make vitamin D itself in sunlight.*

Different types of fat

A fat molecule consists of carbon atoms in a chain. Each carbon atom has two free "arms" which can bond to hydrogen atoms. If they do not join to hydrogen atoms, they make double or triple bonds with next door carbon atoms. In a saturated fat, each carbon atom joins to two hydrogen atoms. A polyunsaturated fat has two or more multiple bonds. Saturated fats can be bad for your heart (see opposite).

Part of a saturated fat molecule.

C = carbon atom
H = hydrogen atom

Part of a polyunsaturated fat molecule.

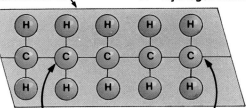

Carbon atoms bond with four separate atoms – the carbon atoms next to it and two hydrogen atoms.

Carbon atoms in a chain.

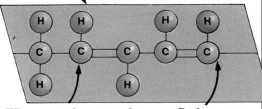

Where a carbon atom does not bond to four separate atoms, it makes double or even triple bonds.

Carbon atoms in a chain.

Saturated fats, such as lard, suet, meat fat and butter, are those which mainly come from animals. They are solid at room temperature.

Polyunsaturated fats, such as corn (maize) oil, sunflower oil and soya bean oil come from plants. They are liquid at room temperature.

*There is more about these vitamins on pages 10-11.

Feeling full

It is tempting to eat a lot of fatty food because when you are hungry it is very satisfying. The reason for this is that you digest fat quite slowly, so it sits in your stomach for a long time, making you feel full.

Fat and heart disease

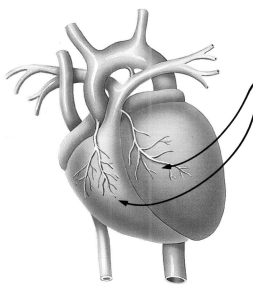

Coronary arteries feeding heart muscle with blood.

All animal foods contain a fatty substance called cholesterol. Your body also makes its own. A diet containing a lot of saturated fat can raise the amount of cholesterol in your blood to dangerous levels. A fatty substance is laid down in your arteries making them narrow.

If a blood clot gets stuck in a narrowed artery leading to the heart muscle, blocking it completely, the heart muscle is starved of blood and cannot pump properly. It may even cause the heart to stop.

Hidden fats

Some foods, such as butter and cooking oils, are obviously very fatty. A lot of other foods contain fat which is not so obvious. Here are some foods with their percentage fat content and the amounts of saturated and polyunsaturated fat they contain. The rest of the fat in them is another type of fat called unsaturated fat. In an unsaturated fat molecule, there is only one double bond.

Total percentage of fat in food.		% of fat which is saturated.	% of fat which is polyunsaturated.
Beef	21%	45%	5%
Eggs	11%	38%	13%
Salted peanuts	49%	21%	30%
Milk chocolate	30%	62%	4%
Hard cheese	34%	63%	3%
Butter	82%	63%	3%
Polyunsaturated margarine	81%	16%	54%

Cutting down on fat

Most people eat too much fat. Here are some ways to cut down.

★ Avoid spreading butter or margarine thickly.

★ Cut fat off meat before cooking. White meat, fish and poultry have less fat than red meat.

★ Grill food, don't fry it.

★ Drink skimmed milk instead of full fat milk.

★ Eat natural yoghurt instead of cream.

★ Look for low-fat cheese.

Vitamins

Vitamins are substances in food which you must have in order to be healthy. You only need them in small quantities and you are unlikely to go short if you eat a range of different foods.* There are about 20 vitamins. The most important ones, and what they do, are described on these pages. The chart on page 46 shows where they occur.**

Vitamin A

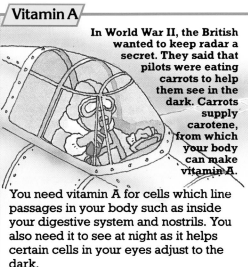

In World War II, the British wanted to keep radar a secret. They said that pilots were eating carrots to help them see in the dark. Carrots supply carotene, from which your body can make vitamin A.

You need vitamin A for cells which line passages in your body such as inside your digestive system and nostrils. You also need it to see at night as it helps certain cells in your eyes adjust to the dark.

Vitamin C

This vitamin is important for skin, blood and general body maintenance. It is also necessary for healthy healing after an injury; for instance, to help form scar tissue.

B group vitamins

Thiamin
Riboflavir
Nicotinic acid

These are B group vitamins.

Some cereals are advertised as having added vitamins. These replace those lost during manufacture. Meat, cereals, bread, eggs and milk are the main sources of B vitamins.

The B group vitamins were originally thought to be one substance. It was then discovered that there are at least 12 different substances involved. Some B vitamins help release energy from food. Others help to make healthy blood and nerves.

Extra vitamin B6 may help women who get depressed and tense before their periods. Doctors do not know why this is, but it seems to work.

Vitamin D – the sunlight vitamin

Many old paintings show babies with rickets, so it must have been a common disease.

Some Ancient Egyptians suffered from rickets. 5,000 year old skeletons found in the Pyramids had bent bones.

You need vitamin D for strong bones. Your body makes it when sunlight falls on your skin. Adults can make all they need but growing children need extra from foods such as eggs, margarine and oily fish such as sardines. If children do not get enough, their bones do not harden properly and become bent. This is called rickets.

*People with coeliac disease may have vitamin deficiencies. See page 41.

**There is a recipe for a salad high in vitamins on page 48.

In the 18th century, more sailors died of vitamin C deficiency, called scurvy, than were drowned or killed in battle.

HISTORY BOOK

Vitamin C is found in fruit, green vegetables, potatoes and tomatoes.

A few centuries ago, nearly everyone went short of vitamin C in the winter when fresh fruit and vegetables were out of season. Nowadays these foods can be frozen, imported from other countries or grown in greenhouses in the winter.

Vitamin E

This vitamin protects other valuable body chemicals. It also makes your blood more efficient in carrying oxygen around your body.

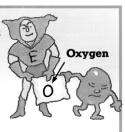

Oxygen

Vitamin K

You need vitamin K to help your blood clot. Without it you would bleed to death when you cut yourself. Your body can make a certain amount of this vitamin itself and it is rare to be deficient.

Vitamin C and the common cold

Some people believe that if you take a massive dose of vitamin C each day, the same as eating 12 oranges, you will not catch colds.

Unfortunately, this has not been proved. Instead, it has been shown that large doses of vitamin C taken regularly are bad for you.

Do you need vitamin pills?

If you only ate sausages, beans and chocolate biscuits you would run short of vitamins.

You are unlikely to need vitamin pills regularly unless you only eat a limited range of food, for example if you are on certain sorts of diet.* You may need them during or after a long illness when you cannot eat or do not want proper meals. Also, some drugs, such as aspirin, destroy vitamin C.

Too many vitamins

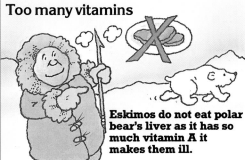

Eskimos do not eat polar bear's liver as it has so much vitamin A it makes them ill.

If you eat more vitamins than you need, you get rid of some of them when you go to the toilet. Your body stores the rest. If you regularly eat large quantities of vitamins, these stores can get dangerously high. This is extremely unlikely to happen unless you take massive doses of vitamin pills.

11

*There is more about safe dieting on pages 42-43.

Minerals

Minerals such as iron, calcium and salt are present in the soil. Plants absorb minerals through their roots. Because you only need small quantities of minerals you are unlikely to run short of them as long as your diet is varied.

You need about 20 different minerals. Some work with vitamins or proteins. Here are the four main reasons why you need them.

1 Building bones and teeth

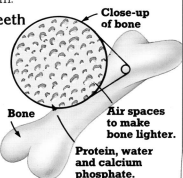

Close-up of bone

Bone

Air spaces to make bone lighter.

Protein, water and calcium phosphate.

Bones consist of a mesh of protein and water, filled in with hard calcium phosphate. This is made up of two materials – calcium and a little phosphorus. Calcium is found mainly in milk, cheese, cereals and vegetables. You also need vitamin D to make bones.

Teeth are made up mainly of calcium but you need another mineral called fluoride for the enamel coating. Fluoride is found in the water supply in some places and is added to it in others to help prevent tooth decay.* Tea and fish contain fluoride.

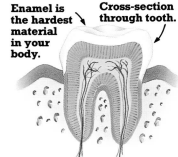

Enamel is the hardest material in your body.

Cross-section through tooth.

12 year olds need about 700mg (0.02oz) of calcium a day. This is roughly the amount in three glasses of milk, 16 large slices of bread, four plates of spinach or 85g (3oz) of hard cheese. You get your calcium from a mixture of different foods, though.

A new baby's bones are quite soft. Calcium to harden them comes from milk in the first few years of life.

A man's body contains about 1,200g (2.5lb) of calcium. This is the amount of calcium found in 1,065 litres (1,875 pints) of milk or 148kg (326lbs) of cheese.

2 Blood

You need iron for the substance which colours your blood red and carries oxygen round your body. This is called haemoglobin and it is made of protein and iron.

> Black treacle
> Cocoa powder
> Pig's liver
> Curry powder

The foods above contain a lot of iron, but you probably do not eat them very often, and only in small quantities.

> 113g. (4oz) roast beef
> 57g. (2oz) wholemeal bread
> 113g. (4oz) digestive biscuits
> 28g. (1oz) iron enriched cereal
> 85g (3oz) beefburgers
> 142g. (5oz) beef sausages
> 198g. (7oz) pork sausages
> 71g. (2.5oz) sardines
> 113g. (4oz) peanuts
> 57g. (2oz) almonds
> 85g. (3oz) baked beans on toast
> 43g. (1.5oz) dried figs

A 12 year old needs about 12mg (0.0004oz) of iron a day. Any six of the above things will supply this. These foods contain less iron than those at the top of the list, but you probably eat more of them.

For healthy blood, you also need the minerals cobalt and copper.

*There is more about teeth on pages 39 and 80-81.

Iron deficiency

The mineral you are most likely to run short of is iron. Substances in plant cells, and therefore in your food, can prevent your body from using it.

Vitamin C helps you absorb iron. Here are some suggestions for meals which contain both.

Grilled liver (iron) and cabbage (vitamin C) for supper.

Orange juice (vitamin C) and a boiled egg (iron) for breakfast.

Iron deficiency causes anaemia. It makes you feel tired and listless. You can get iron pills from a doctor. Never take more than the prescribed dose, though, as too much iron can be bad for you.

Trace elements

These are minerals which you need in minute quantities, such as selenium, chromium, molybdenum and silicon. There is very little risk of deficiency.

3 Cell regulation

Minerals such as common salt (sodium chloride), potassium, magnesium and phosphorus are needed to keep the balance of chemicals in your body cells at the correct level. These are found in many foods and there is little danger of running short.

Salt

You lose salt through your skin when you sweat. Most people eat three or four times as much salt as they need by adding it to food during cooking and before eating, and eating snacks such as salted peanuts. Excess salt can be harmful for some people. There is more about this on page 19.

People living in very hot countries . . .

or working in very hot surroundings . . .

or long distance runners may need more salt than usual because they sweat a lot.

4 Body management

You need iodine, manganese and zinc to control certain chemical reactions that take place in your body.

Iodine is found in fish. It is also added to some brands of table salt.

Zinc comes from wholegrain cereals, peas, beans, lentils and meat.

Manganese comes from wholegrain cereals, leafy vegetables, tea and nuts.

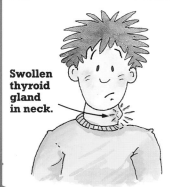

Swollen thyroid gland in neck.

Iodine helps make thyroxin which controls the rate at which energy is released from food. A shortage of iodine causes the thyroid gland in the neck to swell up. This is called goitre.

Fish is a major source of iodine. Goitre used to be common in inland areas before there were quick ways of transporting fish around a country.

13

Why do you need fibre?

Fibre is very important in your diet, although it does not contain any nutrients. It is material found in plants and which you cannot digest. You need it to add bulk to food so that your gut has something to grip onto when moving food along inside you.*

What is fibre?

A plant without cellulose would be like you without your skeleton.

The main type of fibre is a substance called cellulose found in every plant cell. Plants need it to stiffen their stems and hold their leaves out flat. The tough layers round grains of wheat are a type of cellulose called bran.

Roughage and smoothage

Extra pectin is added to jam and marmalade to make it set.

Fibre used to be called roughage, because a lot of fibre foods are coarse and bulky. This is not a good name, though, as some types of fibre, such as pectin found in fruit and vegetables, are quite gluey. This type of fibre absorbs water as it passes through you.

Fibre and constipation

Fibre foods are natural laxatives.

BRAN   LENTILS   BROWN RICE

In the UK, about 26 million pounds a year are spent by the National Health Service on medicines to cure constipation. These medicines are called laxatives. You can avoid getting constipated by eating more fibre.

Eating more fibre

Here are some ways to increase the amount of fibre you eat. High fibre foods are satisfying as they make you feel full without making you fat.

You can buy bran to sprinkle on cereal, or eat high fibre cereals.

Cook with wholemeal flour instead of white flour. Wholemeal flour is made from the whole grain including the bran. White flour has about three-quarters of the bran removed.

Wholemeal bread is made with wholemeal flour.

Ordinary brown bread and wheatmeal bread may have had some of the bran removed.

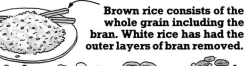

Eat wholemeal pasta instead of white pasta.

Brown rice consists of the whole grain including the bran. White rice has had the outer layers of bran removed.

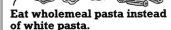

Peas, beans, nuts and dried fruit contain a lot of fibre.

Vegetables and fruit contain fibre, but they mainly consist of water.

Most people get a lot of fibre from potatoes as they tend to eat them regularly.

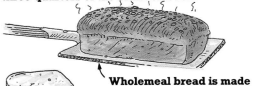

14

There is a high fibre recipe on page 48 for you to try.

Water

Two-thirds of your body is water. Each of your body cells contains water. Your blood is water with minerals, proteins and blood cells floating in it. All the tubes inside you, such as your nostrils, your digestive system and lungs, are moist.

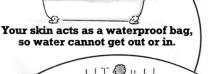

Your skin acts as a waterproof bag, so water cannot get out or in.

Getting thirsty

Salty food makes you thirsty because you need water to dissolve the salt and wash the excess out of your system in urine. Salty snacks are sold in bars to make people buy more drinks.

You can see clouds of water droplets when you breathe out on a cold day.

How much water?

You take in about two litres (three and a half pints) of water a day. One litre comes from drinks and another litre from food. Even dry food like flour and cereals contain some water. You lose about a litre of water a day in urine, and another litre in your sweat and in your breath.

Some bottled water is slightly fizzy. It tastes good with fresh orange juice.

Bottled water

You can buy bottled water which comes from deep underground springs. It contains minerals and is very pure. You need bottled water in some very hot countries where the water supply is not pure enough to drink.

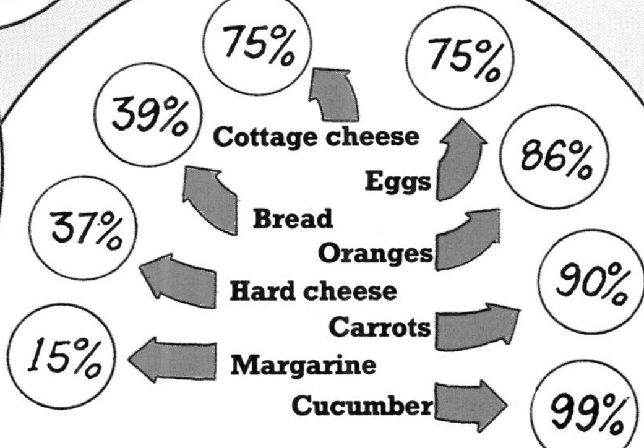

75% Cottage cheese
75% Eggs
39%
86%
37% Bread
Oranges
Hard cheese
90%
Carrots
15% Margarine
Cucumber
99%

Water in food

Food contains more water than you might think. This chart shows the percentage of water in some foods.

Hard and soft water

Hard water contains a lot of calcium. Soft water contains less calcium. Hard water can supply some of your calcium unless you boil it as this gets rid of minerals.

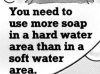

You need to use more soap in a hard water area than in a soft water area.

Healthy eating

How do you know whether you are eating enough of the right kinds of food to supply you with all your daily needs? Generally, if you eat a variety of different kinds of food you will be fine. Below, there are some guidelines to help you choose what to eat. On these two pages you can find out why the guidelines make sense if you want to eat healthily.

Guidelines for eating

★ Buy fresh food rather than ready-prepared, canned and frozen food.
★ Eat lots of different kinds of food.
★ Eat until you are comfortably full – not stuffed with food.
★ Avoid fatty meals and sweet or salty snacks.
★ Do not eat too many sweet foods.

Choosing meals

Eating a mixture of foods will give you different nutrients. These pictures show what Nick eats during the day, and how he gets a good supply of nutrients.

1. Breakfast

Wholemeal bread, margarine and honey (carbohydrate, fibre, protein, vitamins).

Orange juice (vitamin C).

Wholewheat or bran cereal (fibre).

If I have time, I add a sliced banana, apple or raisins to my cereal.

2. Lunch

Milk (protein, vitamins and calcium).

Cheese or sardine wholemeal sandwiches (protein, carbohydrates, minerals, vitamins and fibre).

Fruit (vitamin C).

Tomato (vitamin C).

Sometimes I have a peanut butter sandwich. It gives me protein, but it also contains salt.* I may have a chocolate bar – but not every day.

Processed food

What would your great grandmother have thought of these foods?

Canned soup

Freeze dried beef curry.

Cream in an aerosol can.

Boil-in-the-bag fish.

Powdered mashed potato.

When your great grandparents were young, most food was eaten fresh. Nowadays, you can buy almost any food frozen, canned or packaged in some way so it can be kept for a certain time before you eat it. You can even get scrambled egg powder which keeps for months. Although they might be convenient to use, a lot of foods lose some nutrients during processing.

A lot of food is made to look appealing rather than to be nutritious. This sort of food includes highly coloured, artificially flavoured fizzy drinks, instant desserts, sweets and ready-cooked cakes and biscuits.

You can find out more about these kinds of food on pages 26-27.

16

*There is more about salt on page 19.

3. Tea

When I get home, I have a cup of tea and some nuts and raisins. These are better than peanuts or crisps which contain a lot of salt.

4. Supper

Meat (protein, vitamins and iron).

Potatoes (carbohydrate, vitamin C).

Vegetables (minerals, vitamins).

Yoghurt and fresh fruit (protein and vitamins).

If I fancy a change from meat, I have a vegetarian* meal such as a bean hot pot or a nut stew for protein.

We sometimes have pasta or rice to give us carbohydrate and fill us up. But unlike potatoes, they don't contain vitamin C.

Eating the right amount

A glass of milk would stop my stomach growling.

I eat a banana, some dried fruit, or a large raw carrot to tide me over till my next meal.

If you always carry on eating when you feel full, you will probably get fat.

When you feel hungry, your body is telling you it needs food. It does not tell you what to eat, though. Sweets between meals will stop you feeling hungry but they are not good for you.

Food quantities

Here you can see how much you can eat of different foods to get enough nutrients, without too much fat, sugar, salt etc.

EAT AS MUCH AS YOU LIKE . . .

Vegetables except potatoes, dried peas, beans and lentils.

Fresh fruit.

Salad vegetables (without dressing).

Cottage cheese.

White fish (not fried).

Natural unsweetened yoghurt.

EAT IN MODERATION . . .

Lean red meat and white meat such as chicken.

Hard cheese (not cream cheese).

Eggs and milk.

Fat fish such as mackerel, sardines.

Bread, pasta, rice, potatoes (not chips).

Dried peas, beans and lentils.

Dried, canned, stewed or baked fruit.

Ice cream.

Cereals (especially sweetened ones) and nuts.

Unsweetened fruit juices.

EAT ONLY A LITTLE . . .

Butter, margarine, lard, oils.

Fried food.

Sugar, sweets, chocolate.

Jam, honey, marmalade, syrup and treacle.

Salty snacks such as peanuts.

Fat meat, including sausages and meat pies.

Biscuits, rich cakes, pastries.

Sweet and fizzy drinks.

*You can find out about vegetarianism on pages 34-35.

Things to avoid

Nowadays, doctors can treat many more diseases than they could a few centuries ago and people live 20 or 30 years longer. In spite of this, more people die from heart disease. This is because diets have changed and some of the things people eat are bad for them in the long term. What you eat when you are young affects your health as you get older. Some things are best avoided as far as possible. Here, you can find out why.

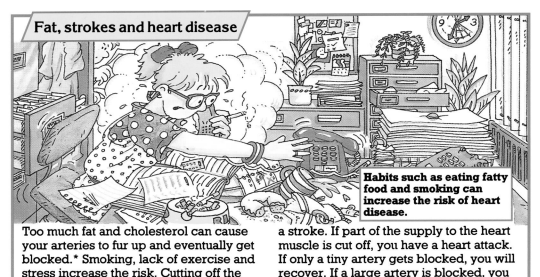

Fat, strokes and heart disease

Habits such as eating fatty food and smoking can increase the risk of heart disease.

Too much fat and cholesterol can cause your arteries to fur up and eventually get blocked.* Smoking, lack of exercise and stress increase the risk. Cutting off the blood supply to part of your brain causes a stroke. If part of the supply to the heart muscle is cut off, you have a heart attack. If only a tiny artery gets blocked, you will recover. If a large artery is blocked, you may die.

What is wrong with sugar?

Even if you cut out all these sweet snacks . . .

. . . you would still eat lots of sugar in these foods.

Although sugar gives you energy, it has almost no other nutrients besides carbohydrate. If you eat too much sugary food, your teeth are likely to rot and you may put on weight. Instead, you can get plenty of energy from food which contains other nutrients as well as carbohydrate.

Being overweight

When you carry a heavy suitcase, your heart beats faster as it has to work harder. Some people carry around this extra weight all the time as fat on their bodies. This puts a constant strain on their hearts. Some people are naturally fatter than others. Unless you are over your natural weight, your heart will not suffer.

18

*There is more about this on page 9.

What is wrong with salt?

> If you stop adding salt to your food and cut down on salty snacks, you will begin to notice the taste of salt in ready-prepared and packaged food.

Most people eat at least twice as much as they need. There is a lot of salt in packaged foods. Nearly all breakfast cereals contain some salt for flavouring. In certain people, too much salt raises blood pressure, which puts a strain on their hearts. In case salt affects you in this way, it is best to cut down on it as much as possible.

Caffeine

> I need a cup of coffee first thing in the morning to get me going.

> I'm dying for a cup of tea.

Caffeine is found in coffee*, tea and cola drinks. It is a stimulant, which means that it makes your heart beat faster and perks you up. The effect of a cup of tea or coffee can last for up to three hours. In large quantities it can harm your stomach lining. It can also put a strain on small children's hearts.

> Coffee last thing at night stops me sleeping.

Changing your eating habits

Here are some ways in which you can adjust your eating habits so you are more likely to stay healthy as you get older.

Less fat   Eat less meat, cream, cheese, butter, margarine, cakes, biscuits, fried food, chocolate and other fatty foods.

More fibre   Eat wholemeal bread and pasta, potatoes, more vegetables, salads and fruit.

Less sugar   Cut down on sweets, cakes, sweetened drinks and other sugary things.

Less salt   Cut down on salty snacks, packaged food flavoured with salt, and salt you add to food you are cooking or at the table.

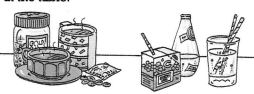

Less tea and coffee   One or two cups a day will do no harm. Drink unsweetened fruit juices and spa water instead. You can try different herb and fruit "teas", too.

19

*You can buy coffee with most of the caffeine removed, called decaffeinated coffee.

Eating habits

By the age of two, you have developed tastes in food which influence what you enjoy eating throughout your life. You can adjust your eating habits, though, if you do not think you eat healthily enough. The main things to remember are to eat regular meals consisting of a wide variety of food in not too huge quantities.

Meals to suit your lifestyle

Most people nowadays need less food than their ancestors because they use up less energy.

People travel around in cars and buses instead of walking . . .

. . . and do less physical jobs.

Many people only have one full meal a day and make do with snacks and light meals the rest of the time. On the right are some ideas for snack meals which are easy to prepare.

Breakfast

After a night without any food at all, your body's batteries need recharging. If you have some breakfast, you will have more energy and be more alert.

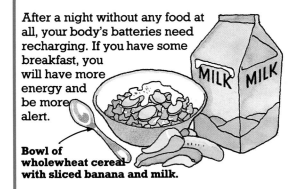

Bowl of wholewheat cereal with sliced banana and milk.

Muesli with grated apple.

Snack lunches

Here are some ideas for quick mid-day meals at home.

Baked beans on toast with grated cheese on top, browned under the grill.

Tomato soup with grated cheese and wholemeal toast.

Between-meal snacks

According to research, most people eat a snack of some sort six times during the day. You only need snacks in addition to good, regular meals if you are very physically active, or if you are growing quickly. Make sure snacks do not take away your appetite for more nutritious meals.

Here are some snack drinks you can make up in a couple of minutes.

Natural yoghurt, with chopped dates and honey.

NATURAL YOGHURT

HONEY

Bacon sandwich

Wholemeal roll with slice of cold ham.

Easy pizza – French bread sliced lengthways, topped with cheese, grilled tomato and ham.

Pilchards or sardines on toast with sliced tomato.

Cottage cheese on rye crispbread with chopped nuts and raisins.

Cold milk whisked into fruit yoghurt.

A whole egg beaten into a glass of fresh, unsweetened orange juice.

On average, a third of the population in the UK eats or drinks something each hour between the hours of 6.45am and midnight.

Likes and dislikes

Food habits are formed at a young age, so small children should be fed as many different kinds of food as possible. If they get used to different tastes and textures, they may be less fussy about food when they get older.

Trying new things

It is fun to try new kinds of food. If you see something you have never eaten in a shop, try it. You may not like it at first, but your tastes might change as you get older.

If you go abroad, try the traditional dishes of the country. Look around shops and supermarkets to see what different food is on sale and how it is prepared.

Making changes

Giving things up or changing a habit is difficult, but there are some times when you may find it easier than others. Take advantage of a time when your normal routine is changing anyway, for instance, when you come back from a holiday, or after you have been ill.

21

Buying fresh food

Several changes happen to your food between the time when it is harvested or killed and when it ends up on your plate. On these two pages you can find out about choosing fresh food to buy so you can eat it at its best, when it has the most nutritional content, or food value.

Fresh vegetables and salad

These vegetables start to wilt and lose vitamin C within hours of being picked, so they are rushed to the shops and sold while still in good condition. Good shops do not sell wilting vegetables.

These keep a little longer than leafy vegetables, but they still taste best and have the most nutrients if they are eaten soon after picking.

Soft fruit

Soft fruits such as strawberries and raspberries deteriorate very quickly. Fruit you pick yourself from a garden or fruit farm tastes much better than fruit you buy, which may have spent a day or more getting to the shops.

"Keeping" fruit and vegetables

Hard fruit such as apples and pears keep quite well for several months in a cool, dark place. Cooking apples tend to keep better than eating apples.

Fruit which needs to be grown in a different climate and imported is picked while it is unripe. It ripens slowly on the journey so it arrives in the shops in peak condition.

Root vegetables such as potatoes, carrots, turnips and onions, keep for several months in a cool, dark place. Potatoes and onions start to sprout in the light, and potatoes turn green*.

22

*You can find out about green potatoes on page 29.

Dairy produce

Dairy products such as milk, eggs, butter, cheese and yoghurt deteriorate quickly if they are not kept cool.

If an egg is stale, it floats. If it is bad, it smells when you break it.

Milk

Milk is heated to high temperatures in a process called pasteurization which makes it keep longer. This kills off most of the bacteria* which turn milk sour, and also any disease bacteria.

Before pasteurization and refrigeration, cows were led round cities and milked on doorsteps. Otherwise the milk would turn sour within a few hours.

Meat and fish

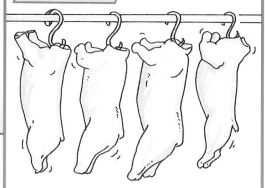

Freshly killed meat is very tough. It is usually hung in a cool place for a few days while it becomes more tender.

Fish goes off very quickly, so it is often frozen at sea. In the shops it is kept in freezer units or packed in ice on display counters.

Buying fruit and veg

★ Choose firm, bright, crisp produce. Old fruit looks dull. Green vegetables are limp and yellowy.
★ Buy them in small quantities and eat them soon afterwards.
★ Fruit and vegetables are best and cheapest in season. Out of season, they may not taste so good as they may have been grown in artificial conditions or been imported.

Buying dairy produce

★ Only buy dairy produce from shops with spotlessly clean refrigerators.
★ Never buy eggs which have been stored in a warm place. They get stale within five days when warm, but keep up to three weeks in a refrigerator.
★ Check eggs are not cracked.
★ Check the SELL BY dates on yoghurt, butter, cheese and so on.

Buying meat and fish

★ Do not buy meat or fish from a shop that is not extremely clean.
★ Avoid packages of frozen meat that contain lumps of ice or liquid that has seeped out and refrozen. If it has defrosted and refrozen, bacteria may have grown.
★ Check fish is firm and moist, the eyes clear and not sunken, the gills bright red and that it smells good.

*There is more about bacteria on page 30.

Packaged and preserved food

To stop food going bad, it usually needs to be treated in some way. It also needs packaging to stop it getting contaminated. Most supermarkets are full of packaged food; either frozen or in tins, jars, tubes or cartons. Here you can find out about how food is preserved and packaged, and whether it affects the nutritional content, or food value.

Why preserve food?

Your food also provides food for microscopic creatures called microbes, such as moulds, yeasts and bacteria. These are present in small, harmless quantities in or on fresh food. In time they multiply.

Fruit juice goes fizzy when yeasts in the air get into it and breed.
As they feed, they break down the food, making it taste and smell bad. They can be dangerous in large quantities as they or their waste products are poisonous.

Bacteria on meat multiply and make it smell bad.

Methods of preserving food kill microbes or slow down their activity.

Below you can see what happens to a loaf of bread if it gets left uneaten.

Harmless moulds are deliberately grown in some cheeses to give a strong flavour.

Freezing

At around body temperature, bacteria can divide every 20 minutes.

Microbes live and breed best in warm surroundings. Freezing inactivates most of them, and refrigeration slows them down. Before freezing, vegetables are plunged into boiling water for a short while to kill off microbes. This also destroys some vitamins and minerals.

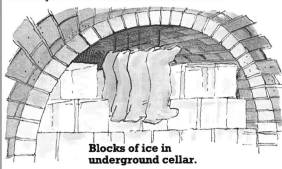

Blocks of ice in underground cellar.

By the end of the 18th century, some rich people had sorts of refrigerators. These were rooms with very thick walls called ice houses, or cold underground cellars. In winter, blocks of ice and snow were cut and put inside. The ice took a long time to melt so meat could be stored there for weeks or even months.

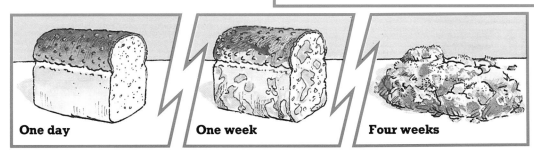

One day **One week** **Four weeks**

Canning

Food is heated to destroy microbes and then sealed in airtight cans to prevent other microbes getting in. Food loses more nutrients during canning than during freezing, though canned food keeps longer than frozen food.

Dent in can may allow microbes in.

Microbes have got into this can, making it bulge.

Do not buy dented cans. The dents may weaken the can and let in microbes. Bulging cans are very dangerous. They show that microbes have got in and bred.

Drying

Fish drying in the sun.

Dried food is hard on the outside, so microbes find it difficult to get in. Drying destroys most of the vitamins, but leaves protein intact, so it is better for meat than vegetables. Drying is mainly done in factories, though in some parts of the world, meat and fish are still dried in the sun or the wind.

Salt, sugar and vinegar

Salt, sugar and vinegar inactivate most microbes. They have been used to preserve food for centuries.

Nowadays, vinegar is mainly used for pickling vegetables.

Sugar is used as a preservative in jams, marmalades and sweet pickles.

Meat is covered in salt and then hung up to dry. This is called curing.

Smoked food

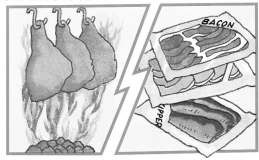

Meat and fish used to be smoked to preserve it. You can still buy food such as smoked kippers and bacon, but the smokey flavour is usually artificial and they last no longer than fresh food.

Date-stamping

To make sure food is eaten before it goes off, many dairy products, packets and frozen foods are marked with a date before which they should be used. Unopened cans last for years so they do not need date-stamping.

You should normally eat food within a couple of days of its SELL BY date.

Food additives

Food additives are substances added to food to preserve it and affect its appearance, texture, taste, smell and so on. Some are natural, such as salt and spices. Others are manufactured chemicals. You can find out here why they are added to some foods and whether they can affect you.

Preservatives

There is more about preservatives on pages 24-25.

A lot of food has preservatives added to it so it will keep on a shop shelf or in your kitchen cupboard.

Anti-oxidants

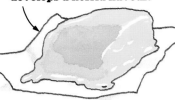

Butter left out in the warm goes rancid and develops a horrid flavour.

Oxygen in the air causes fatty foods to go off. Anti-oxidants such as vitamin E and vitamin C help to prevent this.

Flavourings

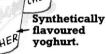

Yoghurt flavoured with real cherries (it may contain synthetic flavouring too).

Synthetically flavoured yoghurt.

Maltol is added to some packaged cakes and bread. It makes them taste and smell freshly baked.

Natural flavourings include oils from citrus fruits and spices e.g. cinnamon. Some flavourings are artificial, or synthetic. A yoghurt labelled "cherry yoghurt" must contain cherries. A yoghurt labelled "cherry flavour" may have chemicals that taste of cherries instead.

Emulsifiers and stabilizers

Stabilizers are added to instant desserts and toppings, to make them foamy when they are mixed.

An emulsifier called lecithin, found in eggs and soya beans, stops sauces such as mayonnaise from separating.

These affect the texture of a food and stop it changing during storage. Substances called polyphosphates are added to cured ham and frozen poultry, to keep them tender and juicy.

Are additives necessary?

The sweetener cyclamate, which is 30 times sweeter than sugar, was banned in the US and UK because tests indicated it might be linked to cancer.

Preservatives and anti-oxidants are necessary to stop food going off. For instance, they make meat products safe to eat if you cannot buy and eat fresh meat. Others, such as food colourings, are less vital as they only affect the look of a food.

Are additives safe?

Some people suffer from dizziness and headaches after eating meals with a lot of monosodium glutamate. This is called Chinese Restaurant Syndrome, as it is used a lot in Chinese cooking.

Many additives used in food are natural e.g. chlorophyll (green), paprika (red) and saffron (yellow). Others are synthetic. All additives are tested before they can be used, but some may have long-term effects not yet known. It is probably best to eat as much fresh, additive-free food as possible. Fresh food is usually more nutritious, anyway.

Food colouring

Fizzy orange drink with artificial colour and flavour – no oranges.

Colouring is added to some foods which lose their natural colour during processing. Others are coloured to make them look as if they contain ingredients which they do not, or just to make them look more attractive.

Sweeteners

Sugar acts as a preservative as well as a sweetener e.g. in jams.

Sugar is added to a lot of food. Other sweeteners such as saccharin are more concentrated. They contain almost no calories and so are put in diet drinks and low calorie foods.

Flavour enhancers

Flavour enhancers can be used when flavour is lost during processing.

Flavour enhancers, such as salt* and monosodium glutamate, strengthen flavour. Salt only works as a flavour enhancer in small quantities. In large quantities, it just makes things taste salty.

Anti-caking and firming agents

Anti-caking agents are added to foods such as icing sugar and powdered milk to stop them clogging up. Firming agents made from pectin are added to some fruit and vegetables during processing to prevent them going soft.

Adding nutrients

Vitamins are added to white flour to replace those lost during processing.

Vitamins are added to margarine so that it contains as many as butter, if not more.

Some foods have nutrients added to them. Vitamins A and D have to be added to margarine by law. When cereals are processed to make breakfast foods, they are heated to very high temperatures which destroys some vitamins. Most manufacturers replace them afterwards.

Allergies and hyperactivity

There are very strict regulations about what can be added to baby foods, in case of side effects or allergies.

Some people are allergic to additives such as tartrazine (a yellow colouring) and sodium benzoate (a preservative). Children with these allergies may be hyperactive, that is, extremely restless, disturbed and difficult. You can find out more about allergies and their symptoms on page 40.

Food labelling

Ingredients: carbonated water, mango juice, sugar, flavouring, preservative E211, colouring E102.

Most countries have food labelling laws stating what a manufacturer must say about the ingredients in packaged food.

In EEC countries, all ingredients must be listed in order of weight. Additives other than flavourings have an E number, e.g. E236 for the preservative formic acid. Flavourings just have numbers e.g. 621 for monosodium glutamate. Some books on nutrition have lists of what the numbers stand for and any known side effects.

*See pages 18-19 for more about salt.

27

Storing, preparing and cooking food

Have you ever thought why you cook food? Raw meat is very tough and chewy and you would probably not like the taste. Baked bread and cakes taste nicer than the flour and raw eggs they are made from. Cooking kills dangerous microbes which might be present. It also breaks down the tough cellulose in plant cells so you can digest vegetables more easily.

Cooking can destroy valuable nutrients, though. So can the way you store and prepare food. Here, you can find out what to do about it.

Dissolving nutrients

Vitamin C, some B group vitamins and some minerals dissolve in water during washing and boiling.

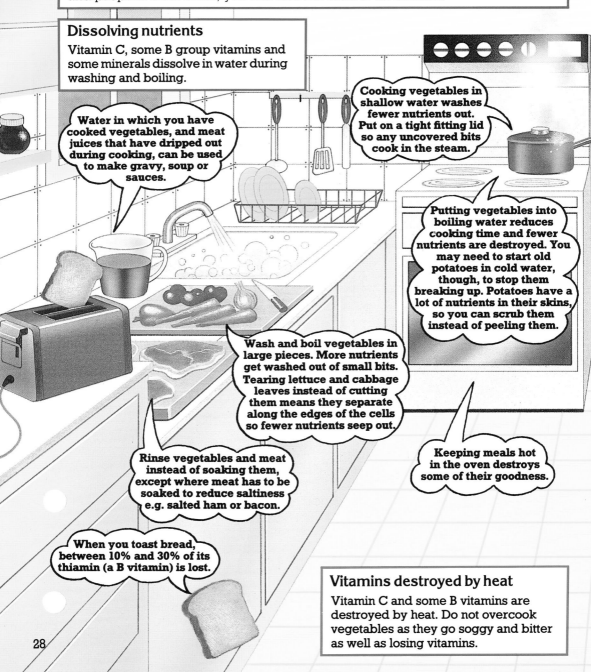

Water in which you have cooked vegetables, and meat juices that have dripped out during cooking, can be used to make gravy, soup or sauces.

Cooking vegetables in shallow water washes fewer nutrients out. Put on a tight fitting lid so any uncovered bits cook in the steam.

Putting vegetables into boiling water reduces cooking time and fewer nutrients are destroyed. You may need to start old potatoes in cold water, though, to stop them breaking up. Potatoes have a lot of nutrients in their skins, so you can scrub them instead of peeling them.

Wash and boil vegetables in large pieces. More nutrients get washed out of small bits. Tearing lettuce and cabbage leaves instead of cutting them means they separate along the edges of the cells so fewer nutrients seep out.

Rinse vegetables and meat instead of soaking them, except where meat has to be soaked to reduce saltiness e.g. salted ham or bacon.

Keeping meals hot in the oven destroys some of their goodness.

When you toast bread, between 10% and 30% of its thiamin (a B vitamin) is lost.

Vitamins destroyed by heat

Vitamin C and some B vitamins are destroyed by heat. Do not overcook vegetables as they go soggy and bitter as well as losing vitamins.

Vitamins destroyed by light

Vitamins A, C and some B vitamins are broken down by bright light.

Storing food in a refrigerator keeps it cool and in the dark. It preserves vitamins destroyed by light as well as stopping food from going off.

Keep milk in the refrigerator. If left out in the sun, its riboflavin (a B vitamin) is destroyed. It also goes sour.

Covering bowls of food with polythene will stop them drying out or passing their flavours on to other food.

Food cooks very quickly in a microwave oven, losing few vitamins.

Bananas go brown in the refrigerator, so keep them in a cool, dark place instead.

Root vegetables, such as potatoes, carrots, and swedes should be kept in a cool, dark place. New potatoes get a sweet taste if kept in the refrigerator.

Storing salads and leafy vegetables in the refrigerator keeps them fresher and retains nutrients.

Potatoes go green in the light. Do not eat them when they are like this as the green is a poisonous chemical.

A pressure cooker reduces cooking time by about a third. It makes water boil at a higher temperature. Vegetables cook more quickly in the hotter water and lose fewer vitamins.

Cooking to preserve vitamins

The lower the temperature at which food is cooked, the longer it takes. The longer food is cooked, the more vitamins are lost. Fast cooking at a high temperature loses fewest vitamins. Some cuts of meat need cooking for a long time, though, to make them tender; if you grill stewing steak, it is almost too tough to chew.

Chemical raising agents

Baking soda and other substances used to make bread and cakes rise destroy thiamin (a B vitamin) in the flour. A cake can lose about 80% of its thiamin during baking. A loaf of bread made with yeast only loses between 15 and 30%.

29

Food safety

If you have ever had food poisoning you will probably want to know how to avoid it happening again. It usually makes you very sick and you feel dreadful for a day or two. If babies, old or weak people get it, it can be more serious. It is caused by harmful bacteria which have been allowed to breed on food. These two pages will help you understand how bacteria spread, so you can reduce the risk of food poisoning.

What are bacteria?

Bacteria are microscopic creatures. Thousands could fit on a pinhead. Some live on you and inside you and are quite harmless. Others are harmful if they multiply inside you or if you eat the poisons, or toxins, which they produce. In a warm room, one bacteria can become several million within 24 hours. Here are the bacteria which are usually responsible for food poisoning.

Salmonella

These bacteria live inside most animals. They are normally killed by cooking.

Staphylococci

Staphylococci may exist quite harmlessly in your nose, throat and ears. They are also present in infected cuts, boils and sores. They produce a toxin which causes food poisoning.

Clostridium botulinum

Just 225g (8oz) of the toxin produced by these bacteria would be enough to kill the whole population of the world.

These bacteria produce a very poisonous toxin in low acid conditions where there is no oxygen. Because food cans provide those conditions, canning involves heating food to temperatures which are known to kill bacteria. Botulism (the disease caused by the toxin) is extremely rare.

Stopping the spread

Everything that comes into contact with food should be very clean. The pictures on these pages show where bacteria can thrive in a kitchen. Read the hints to find out how you can reduce the risk of food poisoning.

Wash dishcloths, tea and hand towels frequently.

The kitchen sink should be kept clean and disinfected and should be used only for preparing food and washing up.

Keep meat, poultry and fish covered in the refrigerator.

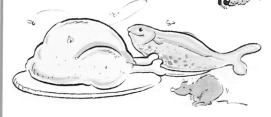

Prevent flies, other insects and mice from coming in contact with food.

More hints to avoid food poisoning

Meat cooked on one day and eaten on another must be thoroughly reheated before being served to kill salmonella.

Wash your hands after removing the giblets from poultry. They will have lots of salmonella bacteria on them.

Cover cuts with clean dressings.

Wash your hands before touching food. Handle cooked and prepared food as little as possible.

CHOO!!

Do not sneeze on food and, if possible, avoid preparing it when you have a cold.

Keep pets, pet food and pets' dishes away from your food.

Keep raw and cooked meat separate to avoid contamination. Standing raw meat on a board may leave harmful bacteria on it. If you then chop food on the board without scrubbing it first, the bacteria may infect it.

Chicken and meat should be eaten within three days of purchase. Cooked stews, pies and gravy should be eaten within two days.

PURR...

Keep all kitchen utensils and everything that comes into contact with food clean.

Line rubbish bins with disposable bags. Empty and disinfect bins regularly.

Wash your hands well with soap after going to the toilet, changing a baby's nappy, clearing up an animal's mess or cleaning out a pet's cage. These are very common causes of food poisoning due to salmonella bacteria.

Use a lot of soapy water for washing up. Rinse everything in clean, hot water and leave things to drain. Bacteria can breed on dirty dish towels. A washing-up machine is hygienic as it uses hotter water than you can when washing by hand.

Defrost meat thoroughly before cooking. If it is still frozen in the middle when it is put into the oven, it may not cook all the way through. You need to be especially careful with large poultry – it can take a whole day to defrost completely.

Eating and digestion

Digesting food means breaking it down into molecules which can be absorbed by your body. This process starts in your mouth and carries on all the way through you. Food travels down your gut, or alimentary canal. The top part deals with digestion, the lower part with absorption and the end part with getting rid of waste.

Digestion

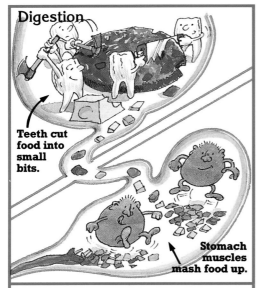

Teeth cut food into small bits.

Stomach muscles mash food up.

There are two stages in digestion. The first stage is mechanical. Your teeth cut food up into small pieces and your stomach muscles mash it.

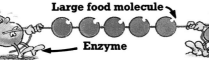

Large food molecule

Enzyme

The other stage in digestion is chemical. Substances called enzymes in your digestive juices break large molecules of food down into smaller molecules. A complex molecule of food is like a string of beads. Different enzymes jerk the string in different places, so finally the string is broken into simple, small molecules.

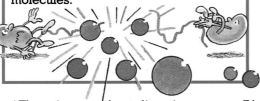

Your alimentary canal

Mouth
In your mouth, your teeth grind, crush and tear food into small pieces. Your tongue mixes it with saliva, making it easier to swallow. Saliva comes from the salivary glands under your tongue and at the back of your mouth. Enzymes in your saliva start to break down starch in your food into a sugar called maltose.

Oesophagus
When you swallow food, your tongue pushes it into your oesophagus. This is a muscular tube which sends food along to your stomach with a rippling movement called peristalsis.

Stomach
Your stomach is a thick, muscular bag. It churns food around, mixing it with an acidic juice called gastric juice, until it is a creamy mixture. Enzymes in gastric juice break proteins down into smaller units called peptides.

The pyloric sphincter is a muscular ring which opens to let the liquid food mixture out of your stomach bit by bit.

Duodenum (top part of small intestine)
A juice called bile flows into the duodenum from the gall bladder. It contains salts which break down fats into small droplets. Juices from the pancreas break down proteins and peptides into amino acids, fats into fatty acids and glycerol, and starch into maltose.

Ileum (rest of small intestine)
The small intestine produces juices which finish off digestion. Peptides are broken down into amino acids and fats into fatty acids and glycerol. Maltose, sucrose and lactose are all sugars which are broken down into glucose.

Food is absorbed in your small intestine. It is about as long as a bus. The ileo caecal valve lets unabsorbed substances out into the large intestine.

*There is more about digestion on page 74.

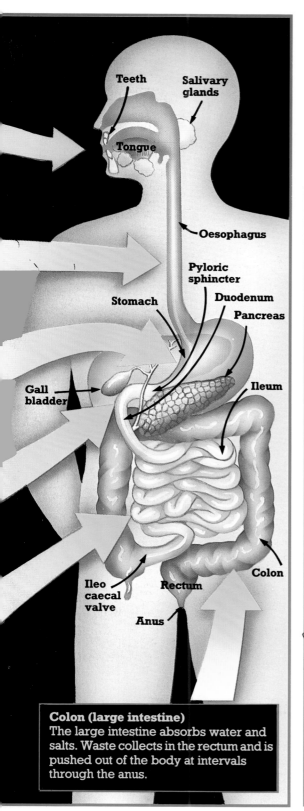

Teeth

Salivary glands

Tongue

Oesophagus

Pyloric sphincter

Stomach

Duodenum

Pancreas

Gall bladder

Ileum

Ileo caecal valve

Rectum

Colon

Anus

Colon (large intestine)
The large intestine absorbs water and salts. Waste collects in the rectum and is pushed out of the body at intervals through the anus.

Indigestion

Indigestion can be caused by too much acidic gastric juice in the stomach. You feel full and your stomach seems to burn. You might get indigestion if you eat too much, because your stomach cannot cope. If you eat very fast you swallow a lot of air. This collects in your stomach making you feel uncomfortably bloated.

How long does digestion take?

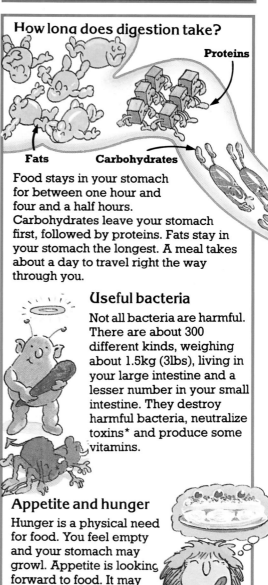

Proteins

Fats   Carbohydrates

Food stays in your stomach for between one hour and four and a half hours. Carbohydrates leave your stomach first, followed by proteins. Fats stay in your stomach the longest. A meal takes about a day to travel right the way through you.

Useful bacteria

Not all bacteria are harmful. There are about 300 different kinds, weighing about 1.5kg (3lbs), living in your large intestine and a lesser number in your small intestine. They destroy harmful bacteria, neutralize toxins* and produce some vitamins.

Appetite and hunger

Hunger is a physical need for food. You feel empty and your stomach may growl. Appetite is looking forward to food. It may make your mouth water. This is your saliva starting to flow.

33

Vegetarians and vegans

Vegetarians do not eat meat. People become vegetarians for various reasons. Some think it is wrong to kill animals for food, or object to modern farming methods in which animals are kept cramped together. Most think it makes for a healthier diet. Some are stricter than others about what they eat.

The word vegetarian comes from the Latin *vegetus* meaning whole, fresh and lively. Different kinds of vegetarianism are described on this page.*

Strict vegetarians – vegans

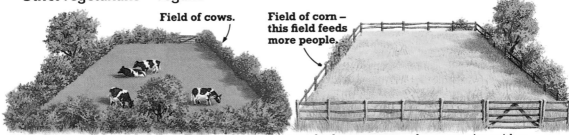

Field of cows.

Field of corn – this field feeds more people.

Vegans are very strict vegetarians who eat nothing that comes from animals. They think that rearing animals for food is a waste of land that could be used for growing crops. A field of grain feeds more people than a pasture the same size with a few cows on it. Besides meat and fish, vegans do not eat cheese, milk, eggs, butter, lard or any food in which animal products are used.

Less strict vegetarians

When you watch lambs playing in the spring, you may forget that most of them end up on a dinner plate.

Vegetarians do not make a distinction between killing a calf, say, and killing a pet.

Less strict vegetarians, called ovo-lacto vegetarians, object to animals being killed for food. They will not eat meat, fish or poultry, but they eat animal products, such as milk, which do not take the life of an animal. They eat unfertilized eggs i.e. those that will not grow into a chicken. Most eggs you buy are unfertilized.

Meat-eaters or vegetarians?

Some cattle raised for veal are fattened up in small, dark pens. This stops them moving about and keeps the meat white.

Battery hens are kept in cages, whether they are bred to lay eggs or for eating.

Some people do not eat red meat such as beef, lamb or pork. This may be because they do not like the look or feel of red meat, especially when raw. They may eat fish and even poultry, though.

Others feel it is wrong that certain animals spend all their lives cooped up being bred for food. The slaughtering process, although quick, may also be frightening. They do not feel so bad about eating fish as they can swim about freely until they are caught.

34

*There is a vegan recipe and some vegetarian recipes on page 48.

A vegetarian diet

You do not need to eat meat in order to get all your nutrients. Here are some sources of nutrients for a vegetarian.

Eggs, milk and cheese have very similar nutrients to meat and fish i.e. protein, iron, fat, vitamins A and D and B group vitamins.

Peas, beans, nuts and wholegrain cereals have protein, minerals and vitamins.

Vegetarians usually eat more fresh vegetables and fruit, and less sugary and fatty food.

A vegan diet

As vegans do not eat any meat or dairy produce, they must get all their nutrients from other sources. A vegan diet needs careful planning and should be made up of a wide selection of these foods.

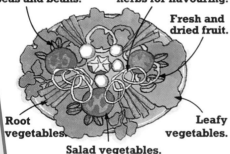

Fresh and dried peas and beans.

Onion, garlic and herbs for flavouring.

Fresh and dried fruit.

Root vegetables.

Salad vegetables.

Leafy vegetables.

Textured vegetable protein in casseroles and "meat loaf" dishes.

Yeast extracts and vegetable stocks in soups.

Pasta, brown rice and wholegrain cereals.

Nuts in roasts, loaves, salads, muesli and desserts.

The vitamin vegans are most likely to go short of is vitamin B12. Until recently, there was no known source of B12 other than animals. Recently, a new kind of yeast has been discovered which makes vitamin B12.

Hindu vegetarians

Cows have not been killed amongst Hindus in India since the seventh century.

Hindus believe that after death your soul comes back in a different living body. If you behave badly during your life you may return as an animal, so Hindus do not eat animals.

Although Hindus will not eat beef, cow's milk and milk products are highly valued. This is because cows are regarded as sacred animals.

Health and vegetarianism

Some ovo-lactarian diets may be no more healthy than a mixed diet, as they contain a lot of dairy foods such as eggs and cheese. These are high in saturated animal fats which can be bad for your heart.*

Most vegetarians consider their diet more healthy than a meaty one, though. Here are two of their arguments.

1. Most cases of food poisoning can be traced back to meat.
2. Animals are often reared cramped together, so infections can spread easily. To limit this, animals are given lots of preventative drugs. Some of these drugs remain in the animal's flesh when it is killed and eaten.

*See pages 8-9.

Health foods

Health foods are thought by many people to be better for you than processed food containing additives, or refined food which may have had some of its goodness removed. Health foods include wholefoods such as wholemeal bread, wholemeal flour and wholegrain rice, and natural foods such as untreated yoghurt.

Here, you can find out more about what health foods are. They also include organically grown food. You can find out what this is at the bottom of the page.

Buying health food

Here are some foods which you may find in a health food shop. See if you can work out from the information in the picture whether they are genuinely better for you than other varieties of food.

Many ordinary supermarkets stock some health foods, at cheaper prices. In health food shops, look for foods which you cannot buy in a supermarket, such as a wide range of dried peas, beans, dried fruits, nuts, pasta and wholegrain cereal products.

Biscuits and cakes are made with wholemeal flour, but contain a lot of fat and sugar.

Brewers' yeast is a good source of B vitamins. If you eat good, varied meals, though, you should get enough B vitamins without taking extra.

Brewers' Yeast

GINSE VITAMIN TABLETS

Pills, potions and cures are usually very expensive and unlikely to live up to the claims made for them by the manufacturers.

Dried fruit and nuts.

Organically grown food

This is food grown without artificial (inorganic) fertilizers or chemical weedkillers and insecticides. Instead, natural (organic) fertilizers, such as farmyard manure and compost, are used.

Plants break down organic fertilizers into nitrates and phosphates before they absorb them. Inorganic fertilizers are already in this form. It is not known whether plants can tell the difference between organic and inorganic fertilizers.

Organic fertilizers improve the texture of the soil, making it easier to dig and for plants to make roots and absorb water.

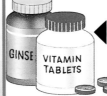

Hoof and horn meal and blood meal fertilizers. Weeding is done by hand, with no chemical weedkillers.

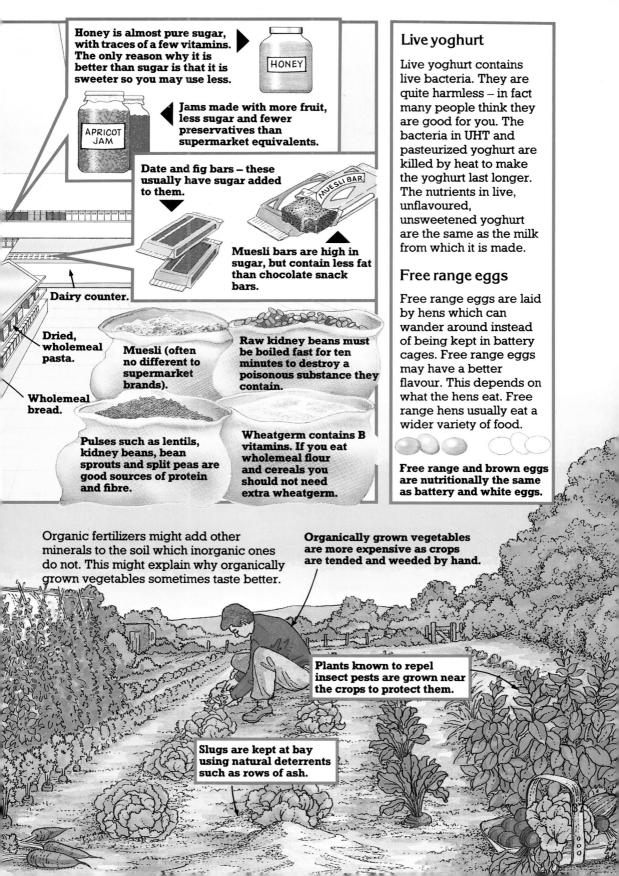

Honey is almost pure sugar, with traces of a few vitamins. The only reason why it is better than sugar is that it is sweeter so you may use less.

HONEY

Jams made with more fruit, less sugar and fewer preservatives than supermarket equivalents.

APRICOT JAM

Date and fig bars – these usually have sugar added to them.

MUESLI BAR

Muesli bars are high in sugar, but contain less fat than chocolate snack bars.

Dairy counter.

Dried, wholemeal pasta.

Muesli (often no different to supermarket brands).

Raw kidney beans must be boiled fast for ten minutes to destroy a poisonous substance they contain.

Wholemeal bread.

Pulses such as lentils, kidney beans, bean sprouts and split peas are good sources of protein and fibre.

Wheatgerm contains B vitamins. If you eat wholemeal flour and cereals you should not need extra wheatgerm.

Live yoghurt

Live yoghurt contains live bacteria. They are quite harmless – in fact many people think they are good for you. The bacteria in UHT and pasteurized yoghurt are killed by heat to make the yoghurt last longer. The nutrients in live, unflavoured, unsweetened yoghurt are the same as the milk from which it is made.

Free range eggs

Free range eggs are laid by hens which can wander around instead of being kept in battery cages. Free range eggs may have a better flavour. This depends on what the hens eat. Free range hens usually eat a wider variety of food.

Free range and brown eggs are nutritionally the same as battery and white eggs.

Organic fertilizers might add other minerals to the soil which inorganic ones do not. This might explain why organically grown vegetables sometimes taste better.

Organically grown vegetables are more expensive as crops are tended and weeded by hand.

Plants known to repel insect pests are grown near the crops to protect them.

Slugs are kept at bay using natural deterrents such as rows of ash.

Fast food

Nowadays, most towns have at least one fast food restaurant, selling pizzas, hamburgers, fried fish, chips or fries, milkshakes, cokes, coffees etc. Fast food is quick and easy to cook in large quantities, so it can be sold cheaply.

Fast food is sometimes called junk food. This makes it sound as if it fills you up without supplying any nutrients, which is not always true. Fast food is not bad for you unless you eat it very often and do not eat a variety of other food.

Nutritious take-aways

Some fast food is quite nutritious. Here are some examples.

Some fast foods and snacks contain a lot of fat and sugar. The red boxes show which you should not eat too often.

Chinese take-away food usually contains a lot of vegetables, and the fat content is low compared to other fast food.

A baked potato filled with coleslaw or grated cheese.

Fries are very fatty, although they also supply energy, protein and vitamin C.

Milkshakes contain a lot of sugar and fat, although they also contain some protein and calcium.

A hamburger made from lean meat in a wholemeal roll with salad.

A pizza with meat, vegetable and cheese on top.

A sausage roll is 36% fat.

Canteen fast food

Many school canteens serve fast food meals at lunchtime, though there is usually a salad choice. If you are going out for a hamburger and fries in the evening, have a salad at lunch so you do not eat too much fat.

So what is junk food?

Sweets, ice lollies, cheap cakes and biscuits, and sweet, fizzy drinks could be called junk food. Next time you buy a can of fizzy drink, look at the list of ingredients. Apart from sugar, it probably only contains flavourings and other additives. The sugar provides energy but nothing else, and it is bad for your teeth as you can see on the opposite page.

Food and your teeth

There is a close link between the amount of sweet food you eat and the number of fillings you need at the dentist. Here, you can find out how sugar causes tooth decay and what you can do to prevent it.*

Sugar and tooth decay

Warmth + moisture + food = lots of bacteria

Bacteria can breed very fast inside your mouth. It is warm and moist and they feed on the tiny particles of food that remain in your mouth and coat your teeth. Sugar encourages the fastest bacterial growth.

Plaque building up around tooth.

As bacteria feed, they produce acid as a waste product. Your teeth become coated with a mess of sugar, breeding bacteria and acid. This is called plaque.

The acid in the plaque eats away at the enamel surface of your teeth. When there is a hole in the enamel, the bacteria get inside. The hole gets larger and the tooth starts to decay.

You should go to the dentist at least twice a year.

When the decay hits a nerve, you get toothache. The dentist drills away the decayed part of the tooth and covers it with a filling.

Cleaning your teeth

Brushing your teeth removes bits of food from them which bacteria might feed on. It also gets rid of plaque but you need to brush for a good few minutes.

Change your toothbrush as soon as it starts to look worn.

Use a toothpaste that contains fluoride.

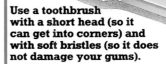

Use a toothbrush with a short head (so it can get into corners) and with soft bristles (so it does not damage your gums).

Cleaning your teeth after breakfast removes plaque that has built up overnight. Brushing last thing at night removes anything that might provide food for bacteria while you are asleep.

Avoiding tooth decay

Try not to eat too many sweets or sugary snacks between meals. Bacteria thrive best on sugar. Savoury foods are not bad for your teeth.

Sticky sweets such as toffees are very bad for your teeth. They stick to them and it is hard to remove all traces.

Have a drink of water after each meal to rinse your teeth and remove some of the food bacteria might feed on.

Did you know..?

★ In the UK, 80% of five year olds have some tooth decay.
★ Only one 12 year old in 200 has no fillings.
★ Dentists extract about four tonnes (four tons) of teeth from children each year.

39

*There is more about teeth on page 12 and pages 80-81.

Food-related illnesses

Some people react badly to certain foods which are normally quite harmless. They are particularly sensitive to, or allergic to, substances in those foods. Other people, such as diabetics and coeliacs, do not have the usual ability to deal with certain food substances. These problems are described here. They can all be treated successfully.

Food allergies

1. Eggs.
2. Cows' milk.
3. Cheese.
4. Caffeine in coffee, coke etc.
5. Yeast extract.
6. Wine.
7. Bananas.
8. Oranges.
9. Certain food additives.

The substances to which people are most commonly allergic are found in the foods shown above.

Some people are born with food allergies but they may grow out of them as they get older.

Other people develop allergies during their lives, but these also might disappear later.

Allergy symptoms

Skin rashes.

Runny nose.

Headache.

Stomach pains, diarrhoea or constipation.

Feeling rotten.

People suffering from food allergies may get rashes, runny noses, stomach pains, diarrhoea, constipation, headaches, or just feel unwell. Symptoms appear up to several hours after eating the food. You may not realize they are due to an allergy as they are also symptoms of other mild illnesses.

Some hyperactive children* who are very restless, destructive and noisy have been diagnosed by doctors as being allergic to certain food additives.

Diagnosing food allergies

Restricted diet.

Different foods added one at a time . . .

. . . until a certain food produces an allergic reaction.

Diagnosing a food allergy must always be done under medical supervision, because it involves going on a strict diet. To start with, the diet only includes food to which people are very rarely allergic. Gradually, more foods are added to the diet one at a time to see when the allergy symptoms appear. The person then knows what foods cause his or her particular allergy and can avoid them.

40

*There is more about this on page 27.

What is diabetes?

Carbohydrates e.g. sugar are broken down into glucose.

Pancreas produces insulin which puts spare glucose into storage.

If there is little or no insulin, glucose has to be flushed out in urine.

During digestion, carbohydrates are broken down into glucose.* The pancreas produces a substance called insulin which stores some of this glucose. People with diabetes (diabetics) produce little or no insulin. Excess glucose is got rid of in urine which requires a lot of water. Early symptoms of diabetes may be extreme thirst and a need to go to the toilet more than usual.

Developing diabetes

Some people are born with diabetes. Others may develop it as they grow older. It can also develop in people if they become very overweight. The pancreas gets worn out having to cope with a large carbohydrate intake.

Treatment of diabetes

Diabetes is usually treated with injections or tablets of insulin and a strict diet limiting sugar intake. Diabetes which appears in older people can sometimes be controlled by cutting down on sweet foods and controlling weight.

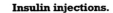

Insulin injections.

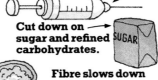

Cut down on sugar and refined carbohydrates.

Fibre slows down carbohydrate digestion.

Less fat to limit risk of heart disease.

Eating fibre helps to control diabetes because fibre attaches itself to carbohydrates in your gut and slows down the rate at which they are absorbed. Diabetics should avoid too much fat and weight gain as they are more prone than others to heart disease.

Coeliac disease

Breakfast cereals made with wheat. Muesli containing oats.

Sausage and beefburgers to which breadcrumbs have been added.

Rye bread.

Bread, cakes, pastries, biscuits and puddings made with wheat flour.

Canned soups containing wheat starch.

People with coeliac disease (coeliacs) are sensitive to a protein called gluten. It is found mainly in wheat, and in smaller amounts in rye, barley and oats. It damages the lining of a coeliac's small intestine, so food cannot be properly absorbed. The foods above contain gluten.

Treating coeliac disease

Many coeliacs grow out of the disease. If coeliacs stick to a diet that does not contain gluten, they can lead perfectly healthy lives. Some food companies make gluten-free bread, cakes and so on for coeliacs. People with undiagnosed coeliac disease are thin and prone to infection. They may go short of nutrients such as vitamins which they have been unable to absorb.

41

*There is more about digestion on pages 32-33.

Weight and weight control

People are all different shapes and sizes. If you look at pictures of models in magazines, though, or dummies in shop windows, they are always thin. There is a lot of pressure on people, especially girls and women, to be slim. Although to be overweight is not good for you, some crash diets are equally bad. People who try to stay below their natural weight are likely not to be as strong and fit as they could be.

Your body bank

Your body's fat stores are like money in the bank.

If you spend as much as you earn, there is none left to store in the bank.

If you earn more than you spend, you can save the rest in the bank.

When you spend more than you earn, you need to use up some of your savings.

Weight, fashion and your health

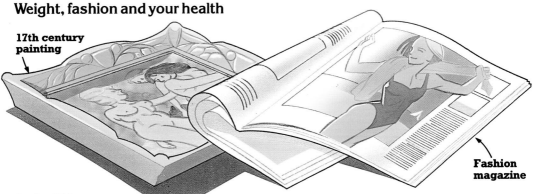

17th century painting

Fashion magazine

In the 17th century, it was fashionable for women to be curvy and fat. Nowadays, the fashion is to be very slim. Fashions have very little to do with what most people are like.

You need to be carrying quite a lot of extra fat around before it is bad for you. You do not need to be as skinny as models in fashion magazines.

Being overweight puts a strain on some parts of your body. An overweight adult may suffer from pains in the back and joints, breathlessness and an overworked heart.

My legs are killing me . . .

Being too thin can also be unhealthy. You may pick up infections more easily and feel weak and tired because you are not getting enough energy food. Dieting can become an obsession.

I haven't lost as much as last week . . .

If you are at all worried about whether you are too thin or too fat, go and see your doctor. The doctor may recommend a diet for you, or may reassure you that you are quite normal.

42

There is more about diets and dieting on page 75.

Using food energy

Some people eat a lot and never get fat. They use up food for energy more quickly than those who put on weight easily. The rate at which you convert food to energy is known as your metabolic rate.

Walking instead of catching the bus.

Dance or exercise classes.

Walking the dog

Cycling to work or school.

Playing a sport.

Exercise can increase your metabolic rate. If you are trying to lose weight, get regular exercise and eat less fat and sugar. Doing any of the things in the picture regularly can increase your metabolic rate, use up calories* and keep you fit.

Using up extra calories

You may notice yourself feeling quite hot after a large meal.

You "burn off" some excess calories by producing body heat. This is called thermogenesis. Slim people probably burn off more calories in this way than people who tend to put on weight.

Without thermogenesis, you would get fatter and fatter if you regularly ate more calories than you needed for energy.

Although fat people appear to have more insulation on their bodies, they may feel the cold more than thin people. This is because thin people keep warmer through thermogenesis. It is like having your own mobile central heating system.

Losing weight

To lose weight, you need to cut down on foods which are high in calories but low in useful nutrients, such as fat** and sugar. You still need your daily requirement of protein, vitamins and minerals.

Cut down on . . .

1, Cakes
2, Sweets
3, Biscuits
4, Puddings
5, Pastries
6, Chocolates
7, Sweet drinks

Crash diets

A crash diet means dramatically reducing your calorie intake for a short time. You should not do it for more than a week without talking to your doctor about it. You may deprive yourself of vital minerals, proteins and vitamins.

—DIET SHEET—
Breakfast
Lunch
Supper

Crash diets are not as effective in the long run as slower ways of losing weight. You tend to put the weight back on as soon as you stop dieting. It is better to make changes in your eating habits which you can stick to for a longer period.

Fad diets

I never want to see another grape in my whole life.

Some diets tell you to eat only a limited range of food, such as tropical fruit or grapefruit. These only work as a way of reducing your calorie intake. No foods speed up the rate at which you use surplus body fat.

43

*Energy is measured in calories. See pages 6-7.
**See page 9.

Food charts

On the next few pages are some charts which show the nutritional value of different foods. On this page you can see what percentage of your daily needs are supplied by such things as a glass of milk or an egg. On the opposite page is a chart showing where most people get their nutrients.

Over the page there are charts showing which foods contain vitamins and minerals, and a reminder of what they do for you.

How much do these foods give you?

The figures in this chart show what percentage of your daily nutritional requirements are supplied by the foods in the left-hand column. The figures are based on the needs of boys and girls between the ages of 12 and 14. Boys usually grow more quickly than girls at this age, so they need more nutrients. The stars indicate that the food is a very important source of the nutrient.

The top figure is for a boy, the lower figure for a girl.	Energy	Protein	Vitamin B$_1$	Vitamin C	Calcium	Iron
Large glass of milk – one third of a litre (half a pint)	7%	14%	9%	12%	★49%	—
	9%	17%	11%	12%	★49%	—
Large slice of wholemeal bread	5%	8%	13%	—	2%	15%
	6%	10%	16%	—	2%	15%
113g (4oz) roast beef	10%	★32%	7%	—	—	17%
	12%	★39%	9%	—	—	17%
Medium-sized egg	3%	10%	4%	—	—	10%
	4%	13%	4%	—	—	10%
57g (2oz) hard cheese	9%	22%	2%	—	★66%	3%
	11%	27%	2%	—	★66%	3%
Medium-sized potato baked in jacket	4%	—	14%	★100%	—	13%
	5%	—	17%	★100%	—	13%
Orange	2%	—	11%	★225%	—	3%
	2%	—	13%	★225%	—	3%
85g (3oz) frozen peas	1%	6%	19%	★48%	—	8%
	2%	8%	23%	★48%	—	8%
Baked beans on one slice of toast	5%	13%	14%	16%	9%	21%
	6%	16%	17%	16%	9%	21%

Puzzle

From the chart above, you can see that if you ate all of these foods in one day you would have met all your protein needs, but not all your energy needs.

Using the information in this book, see if you can think of some other foods which would provide you with some extra energy. (Pages 6-7 might help you.)

Where do you get your nutrients?

The chart below shows which foods, on average, provide people with their nutrients. They show that a food rich in a certain nutrient may not be the main source, because it is not eaten very often.* The main supply of a nutrient may come from another food which is not so rich in it, but which is eaten in greater quantities.

The figures are averages derived from a National Food Survey carried out in the UK. If you are a vegetarian, for example, the figures will not apply to you.

"Cereal foods" in the charts include bread, flour, cakes, pastries, biscuits and breakfast cereals, plus other types of cereal food such as rice and pasta.

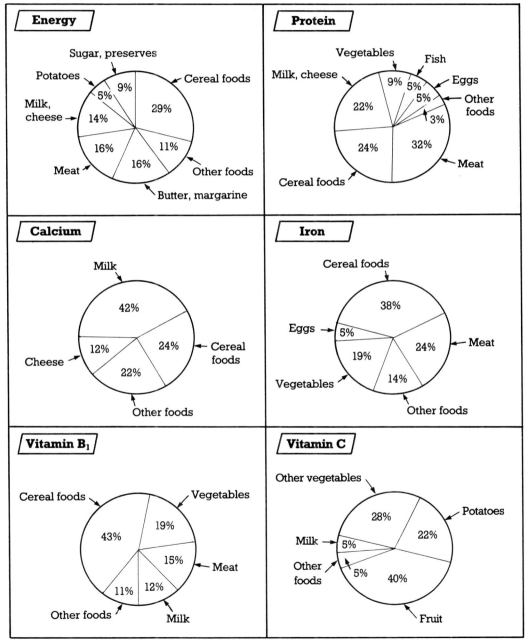

45

*You can find out which foods are richest in different nutrients over the page.

Vitamin chart

Here is a chart showing which foods are richest in different vitamins, and what these vitamins do for your body.

	Food sources	What vitamin does
Vitamin A (retinol)	Fish oils; liver; kidney; milk; butter; cheese; eggs; margarine; leafy green vegetables; yellow fruit e.g. apricots; carrots; tomatoes.	Maintains linings of tubes in body e.g. nose, gut. Keeps skin healthy – helps prevent spots. Helps you see in dim light. Essential for growth.
Vitamin B$_1$ (thiamin)	Pork; bacon; liver; kidney; wholegrain cereals; yeast; soya beans; fish; green vegetables e.g. peas; potatoes.	Helps body use carbohydrate (with B$_2$ and B$_3$). Tones muscles of digestive system. Helps digest protein. Keeps nerves healthy. Needed for growth.
Vitamin B$_2$ (riboflavin)	Milk; liver; yeast; wheatgerm; meat; soya beans; eggs; vegetables; nuts; dairy foods e.g. cheese.	Helps make digestive enzymes. Helps release energy from food. Essential for growth and general health. Keeps hair, skin, mouth and eyes healthy.
Vitamin B$_3$ (niacin)	Liver; lean meat; wholegrain cereals; vegetables e.g. green peppers, peas and potatoes; fish; poultry; yeast; peanuts; cheese; eggs.	Keeps skin and nervous system healthy. Helps digestion of carbohydrates and release of energy from food. Helps regulate cholesterol levels. Essential for growth.
Vitamin B$_5$ (pantothenic acid)	In most foods, especially: meat; cereal foods e.g. wholemeal bread and brown rice; vegetables; yeast; eggs; nuts.	Aids growth and body functions. Keeps skin, hair and other tissues healthy. Helps hair grow. Helps release energy from fat. Aids manufacture of nerve chemicals.
Vitamin B$_6$ (pyridoxine)	Meat; eggs; fish; cereals; green vegetables e.g. cabbage; yeast; wheatgerm and wholemeal products; milk.	Helps body use protein. Keeps skin, nerves and muscle healthy. Assists body functions. Makes hormones, enzymes and nerve chemicals.
Vitamin B$_{12}$ (cyanocobalamin)	Liver; meat; eggs; yeast extract; dairy foods; fish. (Absent in plant foods.)	Keeps nerves and skin healthy. Aids growth. Needed to make blood and new body cells. Helps body use protein.
Folic acid	Liver; offal meats; green vegetables; peas and beans; bread; bananas; wholegrain cereals; yeast.	Keeps blood healthy (works with vitamin B$_{12}$). Aids fertility. Essential for growth.
Biotin	Liver; kidney; egg yolk; oats; vegetables; nuts; wheatgerm.	Helps release energy from food.
Lecithin (choline and inositol)	Egg yolk; liver; kidney; wholegrain cereals; oats; peas and beans; nuts; wheatgerm.	General body maintenance. Helps liver function. Helps prevent build up of fats. A natural tranquillizer.
Vitamin C (ascorbic acid)	Citrus fruits e.g. oranges; green vegetables; tomatoes; potatoes; blackcurrants.	Keeps skin, blood vessels, gums, bones and teeth healthy. Helps heal wounds and bind cells. Helps resist infection. General body maintenance.
Vitamin D (calciferol)	Butter; margarine; eggs; fish liver oils; oily fish. Also produced by sunlight on skin.	Helps regulate absorption and distribution of calcium, so necessary for bones and teeth.
Vitamin E (tocopherol)	Seeds; leafy green vegetables; nuts; wholemeal bread; margarine; cereals; egg yolk; vegetable oil; wheatgerm.	Not fully understood, but you get anaemia if you are deficient. Protects body fats.
Vitamin K (phylioquinone)	Green vegetables; soya beans; liver; oils; cereals; fruit; nuts.	Helps clot blood.

Mineral chart

Here you can see the main minerals which your body needs. The chart also shows in which foods they occur and why you need them.

There are no trace minerals shown in the chart because you only need them in such tiny quantities.

	Food sources	What mineral does
Calcium	Milk; cheese; meat; cereals e.g. oats; fish e.g. sardines; green vegetables e.g. watercress and spinach; sesame seeds; nuts; unboiled hard tap water.	Needed to make bones and teeth (99% of your calcium is found here). Helps blood clotting. Helps muscles work properly. Needed for healthy nerves.
Copper	Green vegetables; liver; shellfish; wholegrain cereals; dried fruit; almonds.	Needed along with iron to make haemoglobin in red blood cells. Helps many enzymes to function.
Fluoride	Tap water, tea.	Needed for enamel coating on teeth. Helps make strong bones.
Iodine	Sea food; cod liver oil; fruit; vegetables. Some table salt has iodine added to it.	Needed by thyroid gland to make the hormone thyroxin which regulates body metabolism.
Iron	Meat e.g. liver and kidney; eggs; beans; lentils; spinach; dried apricots; yeast; figs; prunes; cereals; nuts; cocoa; treacle.	Needed to make haemoglobin in red blood cells which carry oxygen round body. Found in muscles.
Magnesium	Most foods, especially: green vegetables (except spinach); bread; milk; eggs; meat; peanuts; soya beans; sesame seeds; whole grains.	Found in bones and enzymes. Helps body produce energy and use protein. Regulates nervous system. Aids muscle contraction.
Manganese	Leafy vegetables; beans; peas; pineapple; wholegrain cereals; egg yolk; nuts; seeds; tea; coffee.	Needed by several enzymes to help them function properly.
Phosphorus	Most foods.	Needed for bones. Assists body functions e.g. use of B vitamins. Found in all body cells.
Potassium	Most foods, especially: cereals; fruit and fruit juices; vegetables; nuts; meat.	Similar functions to sodium. Helps keep blood pressure normal and kidneys healthy.
Sodium	Most foods, especially table salt.	Occurs in all body cells. Controls body's water balance. Necessary for nerves and muscles.
Sulphur	Eggs; meat; fish; milk; cereals. Present in all proteins.	Helps build proteins and connective tissue e.g. cartilage.
Zinc	Meat; wholegrain cereals; pulse vegetables e.g. peas, beans, lentils.	Occurs in many enzymes.

Some simple recipes

Here are some recipes which are based on the ideas of healthy eating that you have read about earlier in the book.

Country vegetable soup

This delicious soup is a vegan recipe (see page 34 for more about vegans). Chop the vegetables finely for a smooth texture, less so for a chunky texture. Fry the onion for about five minutes in sunflower oil. Add the remaining ingredients, cover and simmer for about half an hour.

Non-vegans could try adding grated cheese to individual bowls before serving.

Ingredients

2 onions	1 pint (600 ml)
3 carrots	vegetable stock
1 courgette	1 garlic clove
2 potatoes	(crushed)
1 leek	Bay leaf
1 green pepper	Salt
2 tbsp orange juice	Pepper

Fresh summer salad

Packed with vitamins and minerals (see pages 10-13), this salad is best served straight from the fridge.

Collect the juice of the oranges when you slice them and mix with a little lemon juice and oil for a dressing. Toss all the ingredients in the dressing just before serving.

Ingredients

Crisp, young spinach leaves (shredded)
Green and red pepper (cut in rings)
Cucumber (sliced)
Radishes (sliced)
Orange (sliced)
Watercress
Thin slivers of blue cheese

Baked bananas

This only takes two minutes to prepare, and is quite delicious. Lay the bananas in a greased ovenproof dish and pour the juice over them. Sprinkle with brown sugar and bake in the oven at 400°F (Gas mark 6) for 15 minutes. Allow to cool slightly before serving.

Ingredients

4 bananas, sliced lengthways
1 tablespoon orange juice
1 tablespoon lemon juice
1 teaspoon brown sugar

Swiss-style muesli

This contains lots of nuts, oats, seeds and dried fruit, all of which provide fibre.* Chop the apricots and dates and mix all the ingredients together. Serve with either milk or yogurt.

Ingredients

Rolled oats or	Hazel nuts
muesli base	Peanuts
Brazil nuts	Almonds
Dried apricots	Dates
Pumpkin seeds	Figs
Sunflower seeds	Apple

Peanut butter dip

Ideal for parties, you can serve this dip with sliced vegetables (crudités) such as cauliflower, carrots, radishes, celery, mushrooms and peppers. The dip is full of protein (see page 4).

Ingredients

Medium jar of crunchy peanut butter
2 cloves garlic (crushed)
1 teaspoon tabasco sauce
1 teaspoon lemon juice

Gourmet hints

★ Add sliced almonds to potatoes before serving.

★ Green vegetables such as brussel sprouts are delicious if you add a little mustard and lemon juice before serving.

★ Keep sliced fruit such as apple and banana fresh by sprinkling with lemon juice.

★ Keep the water in which you have cooked vegetables. You can use it as vegetable stock.

*You can find out why fibre is good for you on page 14.

YOU & YOUR
FITNESS
& HEALTH

Kate Fraser and Judy Tatchell

Consultant editor:
Paul McNaught-Davis

Designed by Sue Mims

CONTENTS

Edited by Cheryl Evans
Illustrated by Brenda Haw, Kuo Kang Chen, Chris Lyon and Adam Willis

What are fitness and health?

The following section of the book tells you how you can keep yourself really fit. Fitness refers to how much you can do with your body. You can find out how to train your body to do more and become stronger and more supple. Keeping fit can be fun. All the activities in the picture below will help you to keep fit.

Later in the book, you can read about how to look after your body to keep yourself healthy. Being healthy means your body is in good working order and ready for anything.

You probably already enjoy doing things that help keep you fit.

Exercise

One of the most important needs of your body is exercise. You can read about what happens when you exercise on pages 52-55. Regular exercise helps your body in three ways. It affects how well your muscles work (strength), your ability to keep going (stamina) and how flexible your body is (suppleness).

Stamina

If you have a lot of stamina you can probably run a long way or climb a long flight of stairs without getting puffed.

When you exercise, your body uses energy to keep itself going. To improve your stamina, you have to train your body to become more efficient and use less energy for the same amount of work. You can read all about this on pages 56-59.

Strength

Your bones are connected by muscles which you use when you move around, exercise, lift things and so on. Strength is the amount of force a muscle, or a group of muscles, can produce.

Different sports and fitness activities strengthen some muscles more than others. You can read about how your muscles work and how to improve them on pages 60-63.

Suppleness

If you are supple, you find it easy to bend, stretch and twist into different positions. Being supple is an important part of fitness as it affects the way you move when you exercise and lowers the risk of hurting yourself.

Some people can be very strong with lots of stamina but very little suppleness. You can read about suppleness on pages 64-67.

Keeping healthy

As well as regular exercise, your body has other major needs which are described on this page.

Food

Your body needs food to help it grow and repair itself and to provide energy to keep you going. You can read about the different kinds of foods you need in order to stay healthy and how your body uses them on pages 72-75.*

Body care

Keeping yourself clean is an important part of staying healthy. It prevents the growth and spread of germs. It also helps prevent such things as certain skin disorders and tooth decay. You can read about how different parts of your body work including your skin, hair, teeth and eyes and how to clean and care for them on pages 76-85.

Posture

Your posture, or how you hold yourself when you stand, sit and move, can affect your digestion and feelings of energy or tension. It can also help prevent backache. You can read about this on pages 86-87.

Sleep and relaxation

Sleep is vital to your system. It gives your body time to grow, repair and refresh itself. Relaxation is also an important part of keeping healthy. It gets rid of tension and allows your body to "unwind". You can read all about this on pages 88-89.

Avoiding dangerous habits

Some people deal with stress by drinking too much alcohol, smoking too many cigarettes or taking drugs. You can read about how these can damage your body on pages 90-91.

Growing up

As you grow up, your body goes through all kinds of changes. Being fit and healthy during this time can help you feel more confident. Pages 92-93 explain these changes and how to deal with them.

Why bother to keep fit and healthy?

Good health means much more than not being ill. Here are some other benefits of keeping fit and healthy.

Looking good

Fitness and health can improve the way you look. Your body firms up and the condition of your skin, hair and so on improve. Good posture always makes you look better.

Feeling good

Being fit and healthy can give you more energy and can improve your self-confidence. Regular exercise helps to relax you and relieve tension. Looking after your body can make it stronger and more resistant to infectious diseases such as colds and flu.

A good level of fitness and health can lower the risk of illnesses, such as heart disease, arthritis and cancer, developing in later life.

*The whole of the previous section of this book is about food and what it does for you.

Why you need exercise

Regular exercise keeps you fit and helps your body work more efficiently. It makes the different parts of your body strong and flexible. It keeps your whole system used to working hard which helps you maintain a good level of stamina. Below you can read about what happens to different parts of your body when you exercise.

Muscles

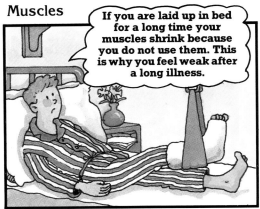

If you are laid up in bed for a long time your muscles shrink because you do not use them. This is why you feel weak after a long illness.

Your muscles need regular exercise to keep them firm and strong. If you do not use them enough they can become flabby and weak. This may put a strain on your joints as they do not get enough support.

Heart

Your heart works all the time pumping blood carrying oxygen around your body. When you exercise, your muscles need more oxygen than when you are less active. Your heart has to work harder. Exercise keeps your heart strong.

Lungs

I need more exercise. . . gasp!

Exercise makes you breathe more deeply and keeps the muscles in your chest strong. It also keeps your lungs used to taking in large amounts of air. This means that you are less likely to get out of breath when you exert yourself than someone who takes no exercise.

Energy, food and fat

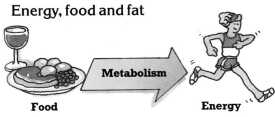

Food   Metabolism   Energy

Energy comes from the food you eat. If you eat more than you use for energy, the excess may be stored as fat. Exercise uses up energy and so can help you burn off fat.

The process of converting food to energy inside your body is called metabolism. The speed at which this happens is called your metabolic rate.*

Energy and exercise

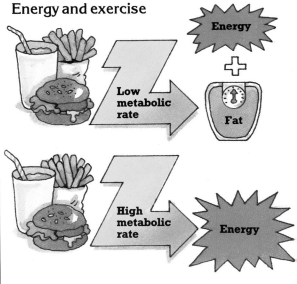

Different people have different metabolic rates. A high rate can provide you with a lot of energy from your food. A lower rate produces energy more slowly and you tend to store more food as fat on your body. (There is more about this on page 74.)

Regular exercise can increase your metabolic rate. A higher metabolic rate releases more energy for you to use than a slow, sluggish one. This can make you feel more energetic in your daily life.

*More about metabolic rates on pages 43 and 74.

Keeping healthy

Exercise can make you less vulnerable to certain illnesses and other problems, such as those shown below.

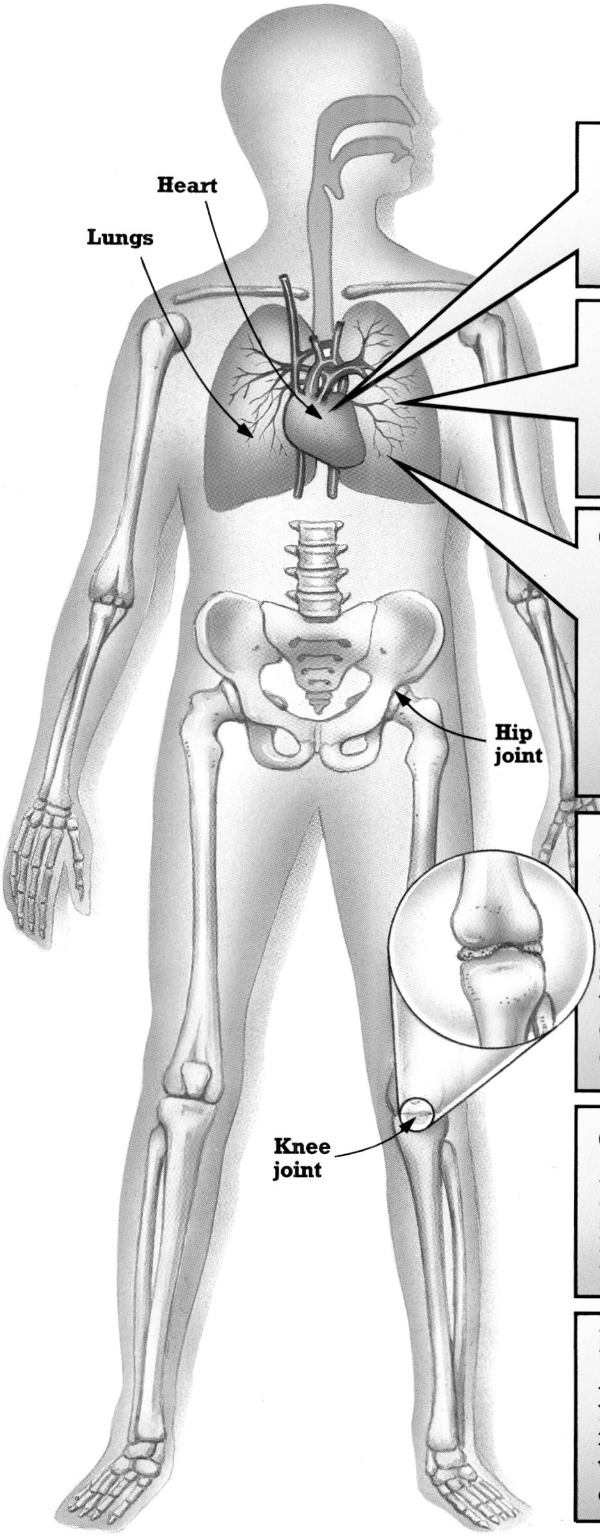

Heart

Lungs

Hip joint

Knee joint

Heart disease

Strengthening your heart can improve your resistance to heart disease. This is the most common cause of death nowadays in the Western world.*

Coughs

One of your body's ways of dealing with chest infections is to cough up the mucus, or phlegm, in your lungs. Strong chest and diaphragm muscles make coughing more effective.

Chest infections

If you have a chest infection, your lungs get blocked up and take in less air. This means that your blood absorbs less oxygen from the lungs. Your heart has to pump the blood through your body more quickly to supply it with oxygen. This puts more of a strain on a weak heart than on a strong heart.

Stiff joints

Without regular movement, joints may lose their suppleness. Certain sorts of exercise keep your joints flexible and strong. Straining your body by exercising too vigorously (over-exercising) can damage your joints, though, which may cause pain later in life.

Colds and flu

A healthy heart can help you resist diseases such as colds, flu and other infections. This is because a strong heart helps to keep your whole system healthy.

Feeling the cold

A strong heart can pump blood round your body efficiently. This helps to regulate your body temperature. People with poor blood circulations tend to get cold hands and feet very easily.

53

There is more about heart disease on pages 9, 55 and 73.

What happens when you exercise?

In order to work, your muscles need oxygen. The harder they work, the more they need. This page shows how oxygen in the air you breathe gets to your muscles via your lungs and blood system.

Exercise makes you work harder. It strengthens the heart muscles which pump blood round your body. It strengthens your chest muscles and increases the amount of air your lungs can hold.

How your lungs work

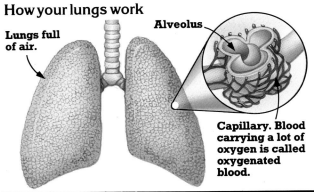

Lungs full of air.

Alveolus

Capillary. Blood carrying a lot of oxygen is called oxygenated blood.

Your lungs are made up of thousands of tiny air pockets called alveoli. These are covered with small blood vessels called capillaries.

When you breathe in, your alveoli fill with air. Oxygen from the air is absorbed into your blood through the capillaries. The oxygenated blood travels through a series of tubes to your heart.

How your heart works

Your heart works night and day pumping blood around your body. The blood travels through a network of tubes, called arteries, to all the different parts of your body. It travels back to your heart through veins.

When you exercise, your muscles need more oxygen, so your heart beats faster to pump more oxygenated blood to them. Your heart itself is a muscle, so it needs more oxygen to do this extra work. You breathe more often and more deeply to take in the extra oxygen.

Main vein carrying blood back to heart.

Main artery (aorta) taking blood from heart.

Pulmonary artery taking blood to lungs.

Pulmonary vein carrying oxygenated blood from lungs.

- - - - Blood carrying oxygen.

- - - - Blood without oxygen.

How energy is produced

Energy is produced in your muscles by chemical reactions between food you have eaten and chemicals in your body.*

A by-product of these chemical reactions, which your body does not need, is carbon dioxide. This is absorbed from your muscles back into the blood.

Your blood then carries it through veins to your heart.

Your heart pumps the blood containing carbon dioxide back to your lungs. Here, the carbon dioxide is absorbed into your lungs through the thin walls of the alveoli and you breathe it out.

*There is more about this on page 74.

Exercise and heart disease

Heart disease develops over long periods when fatty deposits build up inside the arteries carrying blood to the heart muscle. This can starve the heart muscle of oxygen, causing it to stop beating. Lack of exercise, stress and eating a lot of fatty food* may all contribute to heart disease. Exercise gets blood moving swiftly through your arteries, so deposits are less likely to build up.

Exercise and high blood pressure

The force with which blood is squirted through your arteries is called blood pressure. Certain factors, such as stress, smoking, lack of exercise and being overweight can cause your blood vessels to deteriorate. Your blood pressure then goes up because your heart has to pump the blood faster through the vessels in order to carry the same amount to the muscles.

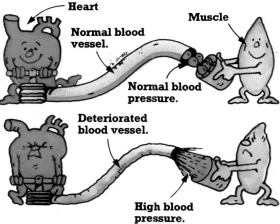

Heart

Normal blood vessel.

Muscle

Normal blood pressure.

Deteriorated blood vessel.

High blood pressure.

High blood pressure is dangerous because it puts a strain on the heart and on the walls of the blood vessels.

Exercise can help since it encourages the blood vessels to open up and grow. Stress and tension may cause blood vessels to deteriorate. Exercise helps you to relax.

Taking your pulse

Artery under fingers.

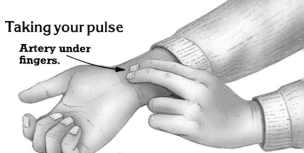

You can take your pulse, or measure how fast your heart is beating, by pressing the artery on the inside of your wrist. Count how many beats you can feel in ten seconds and multiply by six. Everybody has a different pulse rate but an average adult rate at rest is about 70 beats per minute.

Exercise and your pulse rate

INCREASED PULSE RATE

Your pulse rate goes up when you exercise because your heart beats faster. You can check this yourself in the following way. Measure your pulse, then do something strenuous such as running upstairs. Then take your pulse again. As you become fitter your heart gets stronger and can squirt out more blood with each beat. It needs to beat less often, so your pulse rates at rest and during exercise become lower.

Aerobic exercise

Your heart, lungs and blood system together are called your aerobic system. Prolonged, rhythmical exercise such as jogging, skipping or cycling strengthens your aerobic system. This type of exercise is called aerobic exercise. There is more about this over the page.

55

*There is more about fat and heart disease on pages 9 and 73.

Building up your stamina

A good level of stamina increases your energy and enables you to keep going longer during exercise. To improve your stamina you need gradually to strengthen your heart and lungs (your aerobic system) by doing some form of aerobic exercise. You can find out how to test your progress on the opposite page.*

All the activities on this page are aerobic activities. They also help to firm and strengthen muscles.

What is an aerobic activity?

Aerobic activities are those which you can sustain for long periods at a steady, even pace. Your aerobic system grows stronger and more efficient as your body adjusts to the new rate at which you need energy. Many activities are good for your aerobic system, especially jogging, cycling, skipping, swimming and brisk walking.

Other activities which are good for developing your stamina include rowing, canoeing, dancing, windsurfing, cross-country skiing and sports such as volleyball, basketball, football, badminton and table tennis. On page 94 you can check how different activities affect your stamina.

Walking is a gentle form of aerobic exercise. Walk at a fairly brisk pace and wear strong, comfortable shoes.

Jogging is a form of slow running. You can read more about it over the page.

You can skip at home alone or with friends. All you need is a skipping rope and a back yard.

Cycling builds up your leg muscles as well as your stamina. Try to include hills in your route to make you work harder.

Swimming exercises all your muscles and is excellent for stamina, strength and suppleness.

Warming up and cooling down

Before you do any form of exercise you need to warm up your body. This gets extra blood flowing to your muscles. They will need more oxygen when you start exercising. Without it they may become damaged. You can warm up by stretching and relaxing your muscles and flexing your joints, especially the ones you are going to use. There are some warming up exercises over the page.

After exercise, allow your body to cool down gently. Do some bending and stretching and slow down your movements until you are still. Relax so that your heart can get used to beating more slowly. All this will help to prevent stiffness and soreness the next day.

*If you have heart trouble, diabetes, asthma, high blood pressure or any chronic condition, consult your doctor before you take up any fitness activity.

How to go about training

Aerobic exercise means making your heart work a bit harder for a long time. It is a gentle, sustained form of exercise. Your pulse rate should rise slightly during exercise. Short bursts of intense exercise that dramatically increase your pulse rate will not do much for your aerobic system. They exhaust you and you have to stop.

The chart below shows a target zone for your pulse rate during exercise. Take your pulse* before you start. Half way through your exercise, take it again. If it is below the target zone, increase what you do by a small amount each time you exercise. Swim another length or jog a bit further. Increase the distance you cover rather than your pace, so you do not overtire yourself. Take your pulse as soon as you finish exercising to see if it is within the target zone.

Pulse rate chart

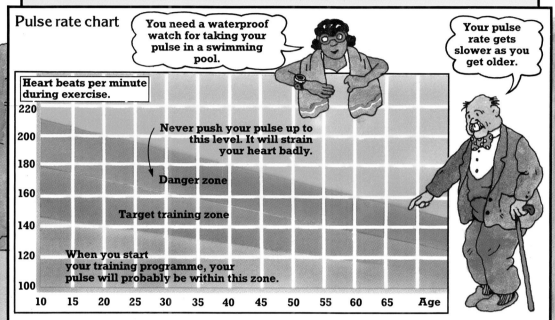

You need a waterproof watch for taking your pulse in a swimming pool.

Your pulse rate gets slower as you get older.

Heart beats per minute during exercise.

Never push your pulse up to this level. It will strain your heart badly.

Danger zone

Target training zone

When you start your training programme, your pulse will probably be within this zone.

Age

As your stamina increases, you will be able to do the same amount of exercise for less effort. You need to do more to keep your pulse rate in the target zone and for your progress to continue.

If your pulse goes into the danger zone while exercising, stop and let it fall. You are working too hard (over-exercising). This will not improve your stamina and it can be dangerous.

Basic equipment

When you are exercising you need to keep warm. You tire more easily when you are cold as your body has to use more energy trying to warm you up. The supply of blood to your muscles may be reduced, causing injury. Wear layers of clothing that you can peel off as you warm up.

★ Trainers are good for walking, cycling, jogging, skipping and many other sports.

★ Loose-fitting shorts and T-shirts allow you to move freely and do not rub. Cotton ones absorb sweat. Materials which do not absorb sweat, such as nylon, can be uncomfortable.

★ Track suits are useful for warming up and to put on after exercise, especially out of doors.

★ Cycling shorts have leather patches which prevent your thighs getting rubbed on the saddle.

*You can find out how to take your pulse on page 55.

Jogging

Jogging is a good way to improve your stamina. You do not need any special equipment other than loose clothing and strong training or running shoes. On these pages you can read about how to develop a good jogging style and there are some useful warming up exercises. There is also a training programme to help you keep track of your progress.

How to jog

When you jog, run at a slow, comfortable pace. If you get out of breath or your muscles hurt, slow down or stop to recover. Here you can see how to move and breathe when you jog.

★ Breathe regularly through your mouth.

★ Stay upright – do not lean too far forwards.

★ Keep elbows slightly bent but relaxed. Shake arms from time to time to relieve tension.

If you cannot talk while jogging, you are going too fast.

★ Let your heel strike the ground before your toe.

★ Do not lift your legs too high: try to glide rather than stamp.

Warming up exercises

Before you start jogging, warm up thoroughly. These exercises warm up the muscles you will be using. Repeat each one ten times.

Stand an arm's length from a wall with your hands flat against it. Bend arms to stretch back of legs.

Repeat the previous exercise with your legs bent. This stretches the sides of your calves.

Lie on the floor with your legs bent and palms on the floor. Sit up using your stomach muscles.

Sit with legs apart. Try to touch your toes, keeping your back straight.

Stand with feet together. Jump legs apart, then back together.

Grasp ankle. Pull until heel touches buttocks. Repeat with other foot.

Jogging for beginners

Start by walking briskly for about 20 minutes three or four times a week. Jog for a few minutes at intervals during your walk. Over the weeks, jog more and walk less until you can jog without stopping for 20 minutes.

You can use the chart below as a training programme but adjust it if you feel you are pushing yourself too hard. It shows how to combine jogging and walking. As you increase the amount of jogging, the total exercise time goes down at first until your body is used to the extra effort.

The numbers in the second column tell you how many times to exercise each week.

Minutes spent exercising.		1	2	3	4	5	6	7	8	9	10	11	12	13	14	15	16	17	18	19	20	21
Week 1	×3																					
Week 2	×3																					
Week 3	×4																					
Week 4	×4																					
Week 5	×4																					
Week 6	×4																					

Walk for 1 minute.　　　**Jog for 1 minute.**

Safety hints

Try to jog on softer ground, such as turf rather than concrete.

If you live in a town or city, try to jog early before the air gets filled with smoke and fumes.

If you jog at night, wear white or reflective clothing so that you can be seen.

Running shoes and trainers

Here are some hints on buying running shoes or trainers.

★ Short shoelaces are better than long ones which you might trip over.

★ There should be about 1cm (a third of an inch) between your toes and the end of the shoe. This gives your feet space to expand when they get hot.

★ Avoid plastic shoes. Your feet may get too hot.

★ Avoid shoes with heel tabs. They may rub against your ankles.

Heel tab

★ Get shoes with thick, cushioned soles to protect your feet.

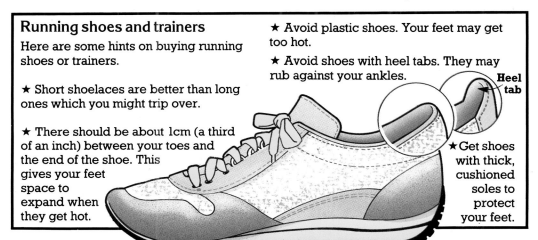

How your muscles work

You have over 600 muscles in your body. You use them to move, breathe and even to stand still. On these pages you can read about how muscles work and how to make them stronger.

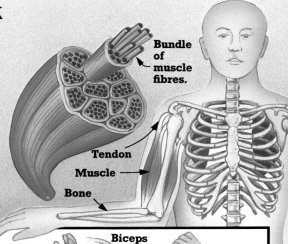

Bundle of muscle fibres.

Tendon

Muscle

Bone

What is a muscle made of?

The muscles you use to control your movements consist of bundles of long, thin cells called fibres. A muscle is attached to a bone at each end by a flexible cord or sheet called a tendon.

What happens when you move?

Relaxed fibres.

Contracted fibres.

Biceps
Triceps

The harder you exert a muscle, the more fibres you use and the more it will bulge out.

When your muscles are relaxed, the fibres are relatively soft. When you want to move, your brain sends signals to the fibres in the muscles you need to control.

The signals tell each fibre to shrink in length, or contract. The whole muscle becomes firmer, shorter and fatter. The bone it is attached to is forced to move.

Most muscles which you use to move are arranged in pairs. For example, the biceps contracts and the triceps relaxes to bend your arm. The opposite happens to straighten it.

Types of muscle fibre

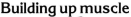

Athletes such as javelin throwers and sprinters need lots of fast twitch fibres to give them short bursts of strength.

You have two kinds of muscle fibre. The kind which provide immediate strength in short bursts are called fast twitch fibres. These contain a form of stored energy called ATP. This enables them to work without using oxygen, or anaerobically.

Slow twitch fibres use energy at a slower rate, so you use them for activities which require stamina. They work aerobically, that is by converting oxygen and nutrients in your blood to energy.

Building up muscle

To develop muscles, you need to make them work hard for a short time. The size of the fibres increases to cope with the extra work. For instance, you can build muscles in your arms and shoulders by doing press-ups. Other methods include swimming, rowing and training with weights in gymnasiums on specially designed equipment.* To build muscles, you normally need to work them harder than in aerobic exercise (see pages 56-57).

60

*You can read about ways to strengthen your muscles over the page.

How muscles affect your shape

If you do not exercise your muscles they become weaker and flabby. They may shrink in size. This affects the shape of your body.

Weak muscles

It is easy to confuse weak muscles with fat.

Weak stomach muscles cannot hold your internal organs in place, which gives you a pot belly. This pulls on the spine and may cause back problems. It also encourages bad posture which affects your appearance.

Strong stomach muscles pull the flesh and organs underneath into shape.

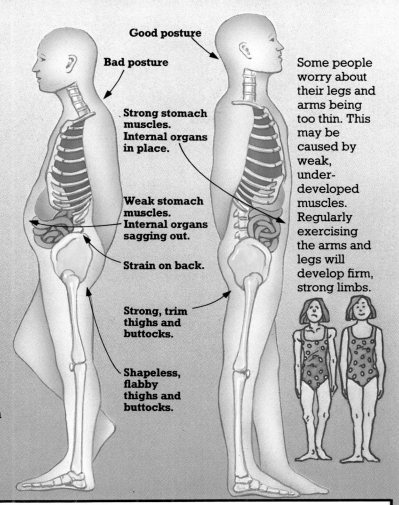

Good posture

Bad posture

Strong stomach muscles. Internal organs in place.

Weak stomach muscles. Internal organs sagging out.

Strain on back.

Strong, trim thighs and buttocks.

Shapeless, flabby thighs and buttocks.

Some people worry about their legs and arms being too thin. This may be caused by weak, under-developed muscles. Regularly exercising the arms and legs will develop firm, strong limbs.

Stiffness and cramp

When you come in from exercising . . .

don't just stop suddenly . . .

or the next morning . . .

you will be stiff.

When you exercise vigorously, your muscles produce a substance called lactic acid. If you over-exercise or stop exercising suddenly, it gets left behind with other waste products in your muscles. This can cause stiffness for a day or two. If you slow down gently, the lactic acid is more likely to be flushed away in your bloodstream.

A feeling of cramp is caused by prolonged contractions of one or more muscles. It may be due to a lack of nutrients and fluid in the muscle fibres but no one really knows.

Proper warming up, a good diet* and drinking plenty of fluid will help to avoid cramp. To relieve it, try gently stretching and massaging the painful muscle.

61

*See pages 16-19 and 72-73 for more about healthy eating.

Getting into shape

Here are some activities which are good for building muscles and improving your shape. There is also some advice about equipment and some simple exercises to help strengthen particular muscles.

Weight training

Weight training. This is different from weight lifting, where the aim is to lift the heaviest possible weight.

Weight lifting.

This machine has stacks of weights which you lift and lower using ropes and pulleys.

You can strengthen almost any muscle group in your body by doing different exercises with light weights. This is known as weight training. You do not need expensive equipment for this. You can use your body weight or books as the loads to lift, as shown in the exercises on the opposite page.

Many gymnasiums have special equipment for exercising different muscles. You can adjust the load on the machine according to how strong you are. This results in a controlled, efficient form of exercise. You should never do it without a supervisor present. Normally you have to pay to use the equipment.

Exercise to avoid

The following types of exercise may build big muscles but can be dangerous.

Pressing your palms together as hard as possible is an isometric exercise, so avoid it.

Isometric exercise

Some muscle-building methods and apparatus make muscles work as hard as possible against immovable objects. This is called isometric exercise. It can encourage high blood pressure and should be avoided.

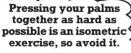

Free weight training
Exercising with free weights (very heavy weights unattached to machines) can easily injure muscles.

Building up your strength

Here are some activities which are good for developing muscular strength. Others include swimming, wrestling, cycling, ice skating, soccer and tennis.

Cross-country skiing strengthens your whole body. It is easier for beginners than downhill skiing.

Canoeing can be exciting and strengthens your upper arms and back.

Riding depends on balance and develops your back, buttock and leg muscles.

Activities such as digging or scrubbing help develop strength. You may develop one arm more than the other, though.

Rowing strengthens your back and legs. They supply the power to pull the oar through the water.

Muscle-toning exercises

The following exercises strengthen and tone different muscles. For the last two, you need to use a light weight. A few books in a bag will do. Start with one or two and increase the load as you get stronger. Make sure the loads are even and warm up properly before you start. Repeat each exercise 10-15 times.

Thighs

Keep knees, hips and shoulders in a straight line.

Kneel up straight. Lean back while raising your arms. Hold this position for four seconds. Straighten up again while lowering your arms.

Triceps

Start with this.

When stronger, try this.

Lie down with your palms on the floor by your shoulders. Push your body up until your arms are straight. Lower your body and repeat.

Buttocks

As you get better at this you will be able to raise your legs higher.

Lie face down, with your arms by your sides. Point your toes and raise your legs, keeping them straight. Hold for five seconds. Lower your legs gently.

Stomach

Sit upright on chair, with legs stretched out. Hold sides of chair and slowly draw legs towards chest, keeping back straight. Lower legs and repeat.

Biceps

Light weight

Sit in chair, holding weights or a light bag of books in each hand. Bend arms and lift bags towards shoulders. Lower slowly. Increase weight slowly over weeks.

Calves

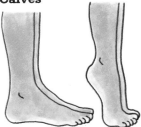

Stand with feet flat on the floor. Rise on to your toes. Lower yourself gently and repeat. You can also do this holding a light bag of books or a weight in each hand.

Weight-training equipment

Here is some of the equipment used in weight training. You should learn to use it under supervision. Never use a weight heavier than you feel comfortable with or that makes your muscles hurt.

Dumbells are short rods fitted with weights at either end. They can be held in either hand.

Barbells are long rods to which different weights are fitted. You hold them with both hands at once.

Light, hand-held weights.

Barbell

Strap-on weights

Dumbells

You can put strap-on weights round your ankles or wrists so your limbs have to work harder.

63

What is suppleness?

Being able to bend and stretch easily is called suppleness. It is just as important as strength and stamina. Lack of suppleness can restrict your range of movement and make you more prone to injury and stiffness.

Most people will never be as supple as trained dancers or top gymnasts but everyone can improve a little by exercising correctly.

How your joints work

How supple you are depends on how flexible your joints and muscles are. Different joints are shaped to allow different movements. The picture shows a ball and socket joint in the hip which allows movement in all directions. The thigh bone has a ball-shaped piece at the end which fits into a socket in the pelvis.

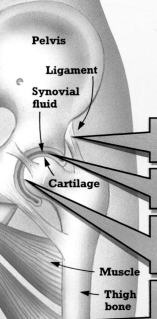

Pelvis

Ligament

Synovial fluid

Cartilage

Muscle

Thigh bone

Ligaments are tough, stringy cords between the bones. They support the joint and limit its movement so that it does not bend too far and get damaged.

The joint is lubricated by a substance called synovial fluid so that the bones do not grate on each other.

Each end of the bone is covered with a rubbery cushion called cartilage. This protects it when you move and absorbs the shock when you knock a joint.

Muscles help to support your joints. The stronger they are, the stronger your joints will be. They pull on tendons connected to your bones to move joints. (See page 60 for more about how muscles work.)

What makes you supple?

The stretchier your muscles and tendons, the more supple you are.

Ligaments do not stretch much but some people have longer, looser ligaments than others. People with so-called double joints have very loose ligaments. This can be a disadvantage as the joint may not be supported.

Regular stretching exercises stretch the tissue surrounding the muscle fibres so the muscles can lengthen. The exercises keep your joints supplied with blood and used to a wide range of movement.

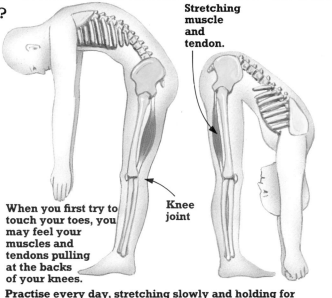

Stretching muscle and tendon.

Knee joint

When you first try to touch your toes, you may feel your muscles and tendons pulling at the backs of your knees.

Practise every day, stretching slowly and holding for about six seconds. Soon you will be able to bend further.

Risks to your joints

If you do not keep supple, the muscles round your joints eventually tighten up. This may cause a feeling of stiffness when you stretch and it puts pressure on your joints when you exercise.

If you force a joint beyond its natural range of movement, you may tear, or sprain, a ligament. You may also over-stretch, or strain, a muscle. If you stretch a ligament over a certain limit, it may not fully tighten up again. This leaves the joint with less support.

When you sprain your ankle, you tear one of the ligaments supporting your foot.

Sprained ankle. ➞

Torn ligament. —

Certain activities such as jogging and cycling consist of the same movement repeated lots of times. Your muscles get used to working in the same direction and stretching the same distance. As they grow stronger, they get shorter. This restricts your suppleness. Exercises such as those over the page help to prevent this.

You can avoid most injuries if you warm up properly and do not over-exercise. Being overweight, carrying uneven loads and bad posture put strain on muscles and joints.

Unbalanced loads put uneven pressure on muscles and joints.

Why keep supple?

Here are some reasons for keeping supple. Remember never to force your body beyond what feels comfortable.

★ Suppleness helps to prevent sprains and long-term damage. It also reduces stiffness in muscles after exercise.

★ Keeping supple teaches you your body's limits. This lowers the risk of over-exercising and improves your co-ordination.

★ Supple joints encourage good posture. Stiff joints can restrict it.

★ Keeping supple can help make your movements smooth and confident rather than stiff and awkward.

★ Bending and stretching help to relax you and reduce stress.

You need to be very supple before you can stretch like this.

Exercising for suppleness

Slow, gentle stretching is the best way to loosen your muscles and develop suppleness. Fast, vigorous movements may cause strain and damage. Some people are much more supple than others and you should not stretch yourself beyond what feels comfortable.

If you do the exercises on these pages regularly you will gradually find you can stretch further.

Suppleness exercises

Below are some suppleness exercises. You can include them as part of your normal warming up routine.* Repeat the top three exercises ten times in each direction and the last three exercises five times each.

Any gentle bending and stretching is good for keeping supple.

How supple are your shoulders?

Hold a ruler and note where your index finger is. Push the ruler over your shoulder and grip it as far up as possible with the other hand. Let go with the first hand. Note where your other index finger is.

Work out the distance between the first reading and the second. This is the distance between your hands behind your back. The more supple you are the smaller the distance is.

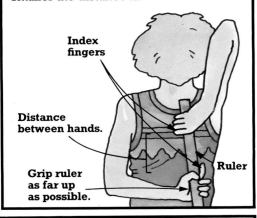
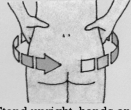

Index fingers

Distance between hands.

Grip ruler as far up as possible.

Ruler

Head rolling

Gently roll head forwards, sideways, backwards and round to the front again.

Shoulder circles

Shrug shoulders. Circle them smoothly back, down, forwards and up.

Hip circles

Stand upright, hands on hips. Swing hips round in large circles.

Back stretch

Sit clasping feet in front of you. Lean forehead down towards feet. Hold for five seconds. Relax.

Leg stretch

Lie down. Clasp one knee and pull gently towards chest keeping other leg straight and flat on the floor. Repeat other side.

Body stretch

Stretch up as high as you can. Then bend down keeping legs straight and try to touch toes.

66

The warming up exercises on page 58 are also suppleness exercises.

Yoga

The ancient philosophy of yoga includes forms of exercise which stretch and relax your body in different postures. It is gentle, non-competitive and can be very relaxing. Below are some beginners' yoga exercises. When you do them, breathe normally and be careful not to over-strain yourself. To learn more about yoga, try to find a proper yoga class.

This is a very advanced yoga position. Do not attempt it or you may hurt yourself badly.

▼ Sideways bend

This helps keep your hips and spine supple. Stand with feet about 1m (3ft) apart, arms out to the sides at shoulder height. Stretch down to one side. Keep legs straight and face the front. Hold for 30 seconds. Repeat other side.

▼ Shoulder stand

Lie on the floor. Lift your hips up over your shoulders and straighten your legs, supporting your back with your hands. Hold for up to a minute.

Sitting twist ▶

This helps keep your spine supple. Sit with your legs tucked behind you. Twist away from them. Relax your shoulders and grasp the arm behind you. Place your free hand over your bottom leg.

Ways of keeping supple

Activities which will help you keep supple include swimming, volleyball, skiing, skating, dancing, gymnastics, judo and tennis.

Ballet is a demanding form of dancing. You need to go to proper ballet classes to learn how to do it.

In jazz, modern and disco dancing, you relax and move to the music. You need a good sense of rhythm.

Ice skating can be exhilarating, and is good for your circulation, balance and posture.

In gymnastics you work on the floor and on apparatus such as the beam and asymmetric bars. You need supervision and careful coaching.

How to stay fit

In order to stay fit, you need to make exercise a regular part of your life. On these pages you can find out how you can do this and about how to develop a balanced training programme. Some people find it hard to stay fit because they get bored with exercising on their own. An enjoyable way to stay fit is to play sports and games with other people.

Team games

If you play team sports, such as soccer and baseball, you can have fun, see your friends and keep in trim at the same time. Many people find it easier to stick to a regular time for playing sports with friends than to exercise alone. Most games are good for stamina and strength and you get a sense of achievement as you improve.

Many team games do not need much equipment. You can easily play soccer using coats as goal posts.

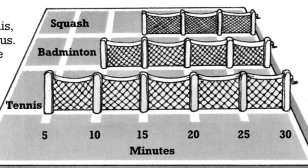

Most sports centres have courts which you can hire for playing squash, basketball, volleyball, badminton and tennis.

Racket games

Games you play with a racket, such as tennis, squash and badminton, seem quite strenuous. However, you have to be quite good before you get much exercise on court. This is because you play in short bursts.* Here is a chart showing how much exercise you get in an average half hour's play. Minutes spent taking up your position, picking up balls and so on are marked by a net. The rest of the half hour is actual exercise time.

Squash

Badminton

Tennis

5   10   15   20   25   30

Minutes

Athletics

You may be able to do athletics at school or with a local club. It is an exciting way to keep fit. If you want to win a race, to jump higher, or to throw further you have a real reason to train and exercise regularly. You will also be able to keep track of your progress.

You need strength for sprinting, shot putting, discus and javelin throwing.

You need to be strong and supple for the high jump.

You need stamina for middle-distance and long-distance running.

*If you are very unfit, slowly build up the amount you play.

Balanced training

Sports affect your strength, stamina and suppleness in different ways. You can see this on the chart on page 94. The picture below shows the different categories of exercise you need to do to keep your whole body in good condition and to achieve a good balance of exercise.

You can use the Weekly Fitness Plan at the bottom of the page to help you sustain a good level of fitness.

Stretching exercises: bend and stretch all your joints every day if possible. (See the exercises on pages 66-67.)

Stamina activities such as swimming, walking, jogging, skipping and cycling. (See pages 56-59.)

Games and sports which you can play with friends at school or in your spare time.

Strengthening activities: sit-ups, press-ups, weight training, swimming, rowing and so on. (See pages 62-63.)

Weekly fitness plan

Use this chart as a basis to work out your own fitness programme. The blue boxes show how often you should exercise during the week.

Time spent per session. ▶	10 minutes of stretching.	30 minutes building stamina.	30 minutes of strengthening.	1 hour playing games.
Day 1				
Day 2				
Day 3				
Day 4				
Day 5				
Day 6				
Day 7				

Risks and injuries

If you play sports or exercise regularly you may hurt yourself from time to time. Below you can read about some of the most common causes of injury and how you can reduce the risk of getting hurt.

Cause of injury

How to avoid it

Sudden muscular contraction
If one of your muscles contracts strongly and the opposite muscle does not stretch quickly enough it gets torn. For instance, you can damage your hamstring (back thigh muscle) when you contract your quadriceps (front thigh muscle) during sprinting.

Warm up your muscles thoroughly before you start exercising. Try to keep your body supple.

Lack of skill
If you are not very good at a sport you are more likely to hurt yourself. For instance, if you kick at a ball and miss, your kicking leg straightens with a lot of force, straining your knee. Also, your back thigh muscles may get over-stretched.

Keep your muscles supple. When playing ball games, watch the ball carefully to help you hit or kick it.

Tiredness
You are more likely to hurt yourself when you are starting to tire towards the end of a game or an exercise session.

You need a good level of stamina to keep you going throughout the game.

Over-exercising
If you over-exercise muscles, they pull on your tendons too hard and the connections may get broken. You need to be especially careful before the age of 15. Until then your joints are not fully developed.

Don't be too ambitious in what you ask your body to do. Warm up properly and increase the amount of exercise slowly.

Running on hard surfaces
You can damage your ankles, knees, hips and spine by too much running on hard ground.

Wear running shoes or strong trainers and run on soft surfaces where possible.

Knocks, cuts and bruises
You may get cut and bruised during games from falling or bumping into other people. You can hurt yourself quite badly by falling off a bike.

Wear protective clothing (pads for football, cycling gloves for cycling) and check all equipment for sharp edges. Try to play against people of a similar standard to you. Stick to the rules of the game.

How to treat injuries

Here you can read about how to deal with different injuries. If you are in a lot of pain, you should see a doctor.

Cuts and bruises

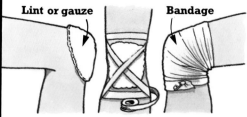

Lint or gauze   Bandage

Wash a cut under running water. Cover a large wound with gauze or lint (not cotton wool). Wrap a bandage round it firmly but not too tightly. If the cut is deep or dirty you should see a doctor for proper cleaning or stitches. If you have a bruise, avoid situations such as games where you might knock it.

Knocks on the head

If you knock yourself out or if you feel sick or dizzy after a bang on the head, see a doctor to check for any damage.

Sprains and strains

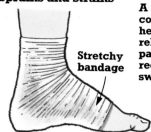

Stretchy bandage

A cold compress helps to relieve pain and reduce swelling.

Sprains cause the joint where the ligament is torn to swell up. Strains feel sore where you have over-stretched the muscle. Lie down and rest the joint on a cushion raised higher than your head. Put a cold compress, such as a cloth soaked in icy water, on the joint. Once you are able to move without too much pain, strap the joint with a stretchy bandage to support it.

See a doctor if it is very painful in case you have broken something.

Fractures and dislocations

Never move someone in great pain.

If someone is in great pain, they may have broken or dislocated a joint. Do not move them and get medical help immediately.

Food and exercise

Do not take vigorous exercise straight after a meal.

Never exercise immediately after eating. Much of your blood is being diverted to your stomach to help digest your food. If you start exercising, your muscles may not have enough blood and will not work efficiently. You may feel sick or faint.

Health risks and exercise

If you have certain conditions such as diabetes, asthma, heart trouble or high blood pressure, you should consult your doctor before taking up any fitness activity. For most of these conditions the right sort of exercise will do you good.

Many famous sportsmen and women, including marathon runners, are diabetic or have asthma.

Eating for health

The whole of the first section of this book is about food and what makes up a good diet. Here is a reminder about the different categories of food that your body needs and what foods you should avoid in large quantities in order to stay healthy.

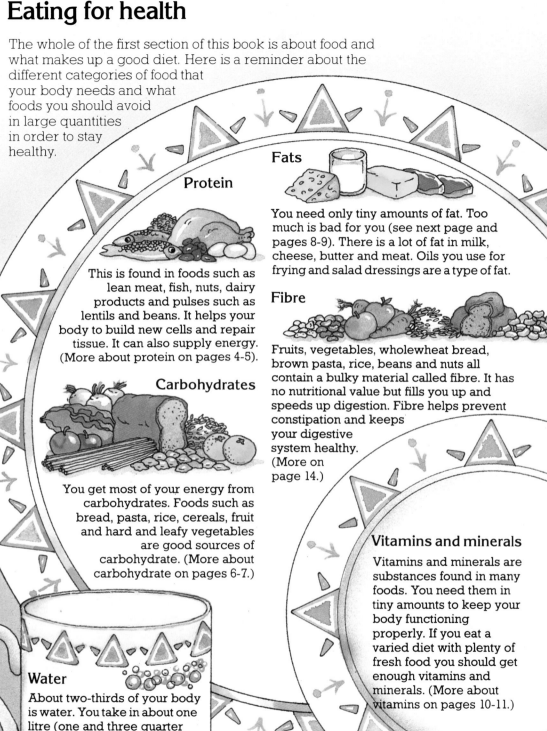

Protein

This is found in foods such as lean meat, fish, nuts, dairy products and pulses such as lentils and beans. It helps your body to build new cells and repair tissue. It can also supply energy. (More about protein on pages 4-5).

Carbohydrates

You get most of your energy from carbohydrates. Foods such as bread, pasta, rice, cereals, fruit and hard and leafy vegetables are good sources of carbohydrate. (More about carbohydrate on pages 6-7.)

Fats

You need only tiny amounts of fat. Too much is bad for you (see next page and pages 8-9). There is a lot of fat in milk, cheese, butter and meat. Oils you use for frying and salad dressings are a type of fat.

Fibre

Fruits, vegetables, wholewheat bread, brown pasta, rice, beans and nuts all contain a bulky material called fibre. It has no nutritional value but fills you up and speeds up digestion. Fibre helps prevent constipation and keeps your digestive system healthy. (More on page 14.)

Vitamins and minerals

Vitamins and minerals are substances found in many foods. You need them in tiny amounts to keep your body functioning properly. If you eat a varied diet with plenty of fresh food you should get enough vitamins and minerals. (More about vitamins on pages 10-11.)

Water

About two-thirds of your body is water. You take in about one litre (one and three quarter pints) of water in drink every day and another litre in food. You need to drink more if you exercise hard as you can lose a lot of water in sweat.

Foods to avoid

Some things are bad for you if you eat a lot of them. Try to cut down on the things shown on this page.*

Sugar

Cereals • Fizzy drinks • Tomato soup • Frozen peas • Mayonnaise • Some frozen pizzas • Corned beef

Sugar is a carbohydrate. It provides energy but contains no other nutrients. It rots teeth and can cause spots. It is very fattening and this may contribute to high blood pressure. You may eat more than you realize because it is in many packaged foods, such as those above.

Fat

Fats which come from animals such as fat in milk, butter, meat and eggs are called saturated fats. They contain a substance called cholesterol. Over long periods, this can cause fatty deposits in your arteries, leading to heart disease.

To prevent this, replace animal fats with vegetable fats, called polyunsaturated fats. Switch to polyunsaturated margarine instead of butter and use vegetable oils for cooking. Too much fat of any kind may make you overweight and put a strain on your heart.

Food additives

Much packaged food has substances added to it to brighten the colour, sharpen the flavour, or preserve it. Many additives are harmless but some people are allergic to certain types and may suffer sickness, faintness and skin rashes.

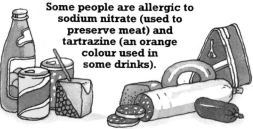

Some people are allergic to sodium nitrate (used to preserve meat) and tartrazine (an orange colour used in some drinks).

Salt

Too much salt may contribute to high blood pressure, circulatory problems and arthritis in some people. Once you get used to eating less salt you may find many packaged foods much too salty.

Coffee and tea

Caffeine only provides a temporary "lift".

Coffee and tea contain a drug called caffeine. This perks you up for about three hours but then you feel more tired than you were before. It can keep you awake at night and make you jumpy and tense if you drink too much.

Hints for a healthy diet

★ Eat as much fresh food as possible. Tinning and freezing food destroy some of its vitamins and minerals.
★ Cut down on saturated animal fat by drinking skimmed milk and eating low fat cheese and white meat and fish rather than red meat. Replace butter with margarine. Cut down to three eggs a week.
★ Boiling food washes out more vitamins than steaming food, which also preserves the flavour. Do not overcook food.

★ Avoid frying food. Grill, steam or bake instead.
★ Increase your fibre intake by eating wholemeal bread, cereals and pasta and eating brown instead of white rice.
★ Try to replace sugary snacks with fruit or raw vegetables.
★ Cut down on tea, coffee and sweet drinks and replace with herb teas and fruit juices.
★ Flavour food with herbs and spices instead of salt.

*See also pages 18-19 and 26-27.

Food and your body

You use the food you eat for energy and to help you grow and to keep your body working properly. Below you can read how this happens.

On the opposite page you can read about weight-reducing diets, why you might feel you should lose weight and whether it is really necessary.

What happens to your food?

When you eat food it gets mashed up by your teeth and stomach into a pulp. Juices from your digestive system* work on this pulp, breaking it down into tiny particles called molecules. These are absorbed into your blood and taken to different parts of your body.

Fats contain twice as much energy** as carbohydrates, weight for weight. During digestion, fats are broken down into fatty acids or glycerol. During prolonged exercise, these are converted to energy. Otherwise they are stored in fat cells under your skin and round your organs.

Carbohydrates are broken down by the body into glucose. When your body breaks this down further, energy is released. If you do not need it right away, glucose is stored in the liver or muscles as glycogen.

Extra carbohydrate is converted to fat. Exercise increases the storage capacity of glycogen, so you store less fat.

Proteins are broken down into molecules called amino acids. These are carried in the blood to all your body cells and rearranged into new proteins to form muscles, hair, skin, blood cells and so on. If you need a lot of energy for a long time or are starving, amino acids can be converted to glucose to provide energy.

Metabolic rates

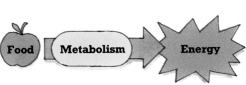

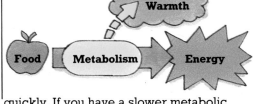

The rate at which chemical processes, such as the digestion and absorption of food, take place in your body is known as your metabolic rate. (There is more about this on pages 43 and 52.)

Different people have slightly different metabolic rates. If you have a faster rate, you may be able to eat a lot without gaining fat because you use the calories quickly. If you have a slower metabolic rate, you may burn up food more slowly and gain fat easily. Some people may have low metabolic rates and still not get fat. This is because after a meal, certain special body cells burn up the excess energy, leaving little to be stored as fat. This generates heat, which is why you might feel warm after eating.

74

*There is more about your digestive system on pages 32-33.
**Energy from food is measured in calories. See pages 6-7.

Losing weight

People come in all shapes and sizes.

There is a lot of unreasonable pressure nowadays, especially on girls and women, to conform to a certain shape. This may make people worry about their weight.

People weigh different amounts because they have different builds. A short, stocky person may weigh more than a tall, skinny person. Men tend to weigh more than women because they have more muscle on their bodies, which is a heavy tissue.

You do not need to lose weight unless you are storing so much extra fat on your body that it might strain your heart and be bad for you. If you are anxious about this, ask your doctor whether you should go on a controlled diet.*

Fat-reducing diets

It is important that you do not go short of nutrients when you are growing. You will feel tired and your body may not be able to develop properly.

Diets where you eat only certain types of food, such as nothing but fruit, may leave you short of nutrients.

If your doctor agrees that you would be healthier if you got rid of some extra fat, he or she will probably give you a diet sheet. A sensible diet gives you all the nutrients you need.

Crash diets

BAD DIET
Starve yourself

GOOD DIET
Cut down on sugar, fat, salt, additives.
Increase fibre.
Eat fresh food.
Vary what you eat.

Severely cutting back on the amount you eat (going on a crash diet) can be dangerous. You are likely to go short of essential nutrients. You may appear to lose a lot of weight to start with but this is mainly water. You may burn up less energy because your muscles may shrink.

Changing your eating habits in the long term by cutting down on fat and sugar and increasing fibre intake is a far more effective way to lose fat than by going on a crash diet.

Exercise and losing weight

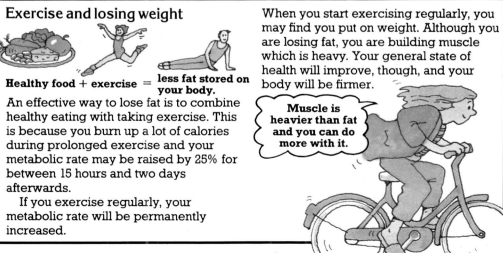

Healthy food + exercise = less fat stored on your body.

An effective way to lose fat is to combine healthy eating with taking exercise. This is because you burn up a lot of calories during prolonged exercise and your metabolic rate may be raised by 25% for between 15 hours and two days afterwards.

If you exercise regularly, your metabolic rate will be permanently increased.

When you start exercising regularly, you may find you put on weight. Although you are losing fat, you are building muscle which is heavy. Your general state of health will improve, though, and your body will be firmer.

Muscle is heavier than fat and you can do more with it.

*There is more about weight control and dieting on pages 42-43.

75

All about skin

Your skin forms a barrier which keeps your body waterproof and prevents infections entering it. You can read about its other functions below. The opposite page shows how to deal with skin problems such as spots, over-greasy or dry skin.

Hair

Fat layer

Epidermis

Dermis

How your skin works

Your skin consists of two main layers: the outer layer, or epidermis, and the inner layer, or dermis. The cells at the base of the epidermis are constantly dividing. As cells are pushed out towards the surface, they die. The outside layer of dead cells is constantly being worn away and replaced with new cells from underneath.

Inner epidermis replacing top layer.

Top skin layer being worn away.

Sebaceous glands produce an oily substance called sebum. This lubricates your hair and skin and stops them drying out and cracking. It helps to keep your body waterproof, preventing germs from getting inside. If the glands produce too much sebum, your skin gets greasy.

Follicle (pit containing living root of hair).

Sebaceous gland

Pores (openings in your skin leading from a sebaceous or sweat gland).

Sebum

Sweat is produced by sweat glands in your dermis and comes out through pores. Sweat helps to cool you down when it evaporates off your skin. It contains dissolved waste matter.

Sweat gland

Sweat

When you are hot, your blood is pumped to the capillaries near the skin surface, so it can be cooled by being near the air. This is why you flush red when hot.

Blood vessels (capillaries) in hot weather.

When you are cold, these capillaries are blocked off so that less blood can reach them and less heat is lost. This is why you go pale when you are cold.

Capillaries in cold weather.

Nerve endings in your dermis sense pain, pressure, irritation, temperature and so on. They send the information along nerves to your brain.

Message to brain.

Nerve

Looking after your skin

Cleaning your skin rids it of dirt, make-up and the old, outer layers of dead skin which can block up pores and cause spots and infection.

 Soap and water are as good as cleansing lotions for cleaning skin. However, if your skin is dry and feels tight after washing with soap and water, use a cream cleanser instead. Massage your skin afterwards with moisturizer.

 Eye make-up remover pads or lotions do not sting your eyes.

 Astringent lotions may help to dissolve grease and remove dirt and they leave a protective barrier on your skin. A good natural one is witch hazel.

Moisturizers put a film on your skin's surface that helps to seal in its moisture. They do not add extra moisture. Use a grease-free moisturizer on greasy skin.

Improving your skin

Here are some hints on how to deal with different skin problems.

Blackhead (plug of dead cells and sebum in the pore).   **Whitehead (tiny spot containing hardened sebum).**   **Pimple (spot which has become infected and inflamed).**

Blackheads are caused by too many dead skin cells and too much sebum being produced. The cells go black on contact with oxygen in the air. Whiteheads are caused by blockages in the sebaceous or sweat glands. Pimples occur when a blockage to the pore of a sebaceous gland causes it to burst. The surrounding tissues become infected.

Blackhead remover

Fiddling with spots can introduce dirt and lead to infection. It is best to leave them alone. If you must, you can squeeze uninflamed blackheads and whiteheads with a blackhead remover, which you can buy. Sterilize it with an antiseptic and wash your hands first.

Oily skin

Oily skins look shiny and the pores may be visible. They may also be spottier than dry skins and attract more dirt.

Oily skins are caused by too much sebum. Use soap or a non-greasy liquid cleanser. Avoid rubbing the skin too vigorously as this may stimulate the sebaceous glands. Remove excess oil with an astringent lotion.

Acne

The changes that your body undergoes during adolescence often cause oily skin, which may develop into acne (dense areas of pimples). If you have acne, wash your face gently with mild soap to remove grease. Gels and lotions which peel off the top layer of the skin may help to unblock blackheads and pimples.

If your acne is bad your doctor may be able to help by prescribing creams or antibiotics, or by referring you to a skin specialist (dermatologist).

Dry skin

Dry skin feels tight and may look flaky. It becomes easily chapped and rough in cold or windy weather. It occurs when not enough sebum is produced, so that too much moisture is lost from the skin. Use a cream cleanser and moisturize the face and throat regularly.

77

Healthy hair

Because your hair cannot feel pain, it is easy to damage it by mistake. If you want to look after your hair properly, you may find it useful to understand its structure. You can read about this below and about why your hair is the colour and texture that it is.

The opposite page tells you what you can do about different hair problems and why they occur.

Your hair's structure

The innermost layer is mostly spongy tissue.

Each strand of hair has three layers. The outer layer, or cuticle, is made up of lots of scales, like a fish's skin. If the scales are smooth your hair looks glossy. If they are rough and damaged your hair looks dull.

Oily sebum from the sebaceous glands makes your hair glossy and supple and affects how greasy or dry it is.

Scalp

The shape of the pit, or follicle, that each hair grows from determines how curly or straight each one will be.

The middle layer, or cortex, consists of strong, elastic cells. They contain a substance called melanin which colours your hair. If you look at a handful of your hair you will see that it is made up of lots of different coloured hairs.

Each hair is attached to a muscle. These can contract and make your hairs stand on end, trapping warmth between hairs when you are cold.

Muscle

Follicle

Sweat gland

Washing your hair

Washing removes dirt, grease and dead cells from your scalp. Use a mild shampoo, such as baby shampoo, as the scalp can be irritated by strong ones. Some shampoos state how acidic or alkaline they are. This is measured as a pH value. pH1 is very acidic. pH14 is very alkaline. pH5 is about right for a shampoo as it is about the same level of acidity as your scalp.

Conditioning

Dry or damaged hair cuticle.

After conditioning.

Conditioners coat the hair shaft and smooth down the cuticle. This makes it easier to comb out tangles. They help to prevent dry hair and to increase gloss. Apply the conditioner to your hair, not to your scalp.

Drying your hair

The best way to dry hair is to let it dry naturally. Pat your hair gently, then wrap it in a towel for several minutes before combing carefully. Hair dryers can damage hair if they are too hot or held closer than six inches away.

Brushing and combing

Wide-spaced teeth

Round ends

Wide spaces between bristles.

Use a flexible, plastic comb with widely-spaced teeth with round ends. Start at the ends of your hair and work your way towards the roots, to avoid tearing hair. Use brushes with wide spaces between the bristles and keep them clean.

Brush your hair gently. Too much brushing can aggravate oily scalps.

Dandruff

This is a build-up of dead skin cells stuck together with sebum on the scalp. It is not an infection and does not respond to the antiseptic in medicated shampoos.

If you have dandruff, try washing your hair frequently and very gently with a mild shampoo. Anti-dandruff shampoos may irritate the scalp. Consult your doctor if your dandruff is very bad.

Greasy hair

Many people have greasy hair during adolescence. Shampoo it as often as it needs, if necessary every day. Use a mild shampoo, as strong brands often stimulate sebaceous glands to produce more oil. If you have split ends, apply conditioner only to the tips of your hair.

Dry hair

If your hair feels dry and brittle, avoid washing it more than is necessary to keep it clean, as this will reduce the amount of sebum in your hair. Use a conditioner. Gentle brushing will spread sebum down the hairs and keep your hair glossy.

Split ends

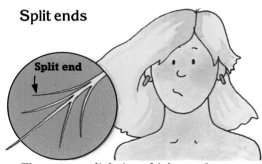

Split end

These are split hairs which may be caused by rough brushing and combing or using a hair dryer that is too hot. To prevent the split spreading up the hair, have your hair trimmed every two months.

Lice

These are little insects which lay eggs and stick them to the scalp. They are very hard to remove. The main symptom is itching. They are extremely contagious so you should treat them promptly. There are several different lotions on the market. You leave the lotion on to kill the eggs, then comb the eggs out.

Dyes, perms and bleaches

Dyeing, perming and bleaching all involve the use of chemicals which can weaken and damage hair.

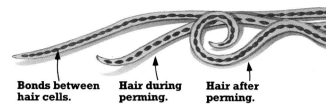

Bonds between hair cells.   **Hair during perming.**   **Hair after perming.**

Perms work by breaking down the bonds between your hair cells and resetting them in a different shape.

Semi-permanent vegetable hair dyes are less harmful than permanent dyes.

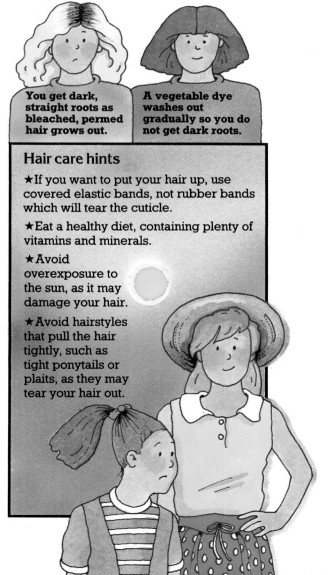

You get dark, straight roots as bleached, permed hair grows out.

A vegetable dye washes out gradually so you do not get dark roots.

Hair care hints

★ If you want to put your hair up, use covered elastic bands, not rubber bands which will tear the cuticle.

★ Eat a healthy diet, containing plenty of vitamins and minerals.

★ Avoid overexposure to the sun, as it may damage your hair.

★ Avoid hairstyles that pull the hair tightly, such as tight ponytails or plaits, as they may tear your hair out.

Healthy teeth

Teeth seem to be tough and hard but if you neglect them they are easily damaged. Below is a diagram of how a tooth is constructed, followed by some of the problems you may get with your teeth and gums. Opposite you can read about how to look after them to keep them strong.*

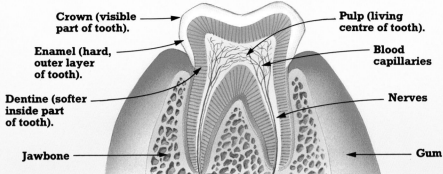

Crown (visible part of tooth).

Enamel (hard, outer layer of tooth).

Dentine (softer inside part of tooth).

Jawbone

Pulp (living centre of tooth).

Blood capillaries

Nerves

Gum

Toothache

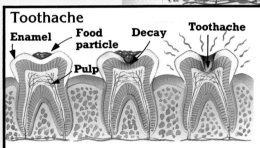

Enamel

Food particle

Decay

Toothache

Pulp

Your mouth contains bacteria which feed on food particles. As they feed, they produce acid which attacks the tooth enamel. A sticky white mixture of bacteria, food and acid, called plaque, builds up on your teeth. As the enamel gets eaten away, your teeth become sensitive to cold, heat and sweetness. If the decay carries on it may reach the inner pulp. If it hits a nerve you get toothache.

   Cutting down on sweet foods and brushing your teeth after meals to remove plaque and food helps prevent decay.

Bad breath

Bad breath, or halitosis, may be caused by tooth decay, rotting food stuck between your teeth, infected gums, smoking, alcohol, bad colds or tonsillitis. There may be no obvious reason. A doctor or dentist can help you track down the cause.

   A good natural way to help bad breath is to eat raw green vegetables such as parsley or lettuce.

Gum disease

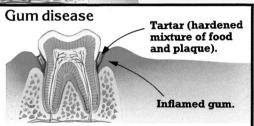

Tartar (hardened mixture of food and plaque).

Inflamed gum.

Plaque which is allowed to build up at the base of your teeth can cause gum disease. It forms a hard deposit, called tartar, which irritates the gums. Diseased gums may feel sore and bleed when you brush them. In serious cases, a tooth may loosen and fall out. Careful brushing and regular dental check-ups help to avoid this.

Crooked teeth

Some people have sticking out teeth, gaps between their teeth, or teeth growing at odd angles making it difficult to bite. Your dentist can straighten them using a light plastic device called a brace. Thin wires from this, attached to tiny springs, are looped round your teeth. Over a period of time, your dentist gradually tightens these wires to pull your teeth back into line.

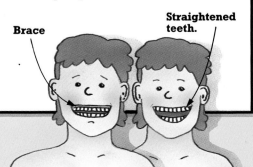

Brace

Straightened teeth.

80

*There is more about teeth on page 39.

Cleaning your teeth

You need to clean your teeth at least twice a day to rid them of plaque and food particles. Try to clean them after eating sweet things, too.

Brush biting surfaces and the base of your teeth next to the gums with small circular movements. Push the bristles into areas where plaque may collect. Do not brush your teeth vigorously backwards and forwards. This may damage gums and wear troughs in the teeth.

Use toothpicks to remove pieces of food stuck between your teeth.

Plaque is difficult to see. You can buy solutions or tablets called plaque disclosers. These go bright pink on contact with plaque to show where it is.

You can clean between your teeth using a special thread called dental floss. You pull it gently up and down between your teeth to rub away the plaque.

Brush upwards on the bottom teeth and downwards on the top teeth, both inside and out, to remove plaque from between them.

Use a soft toothbrush, as hard, spiky bristles irritate your gums. Smaller heads make it easier to brush individual teeth. Change your toothbrush every three months as they wear out quickly.

Many toothpastes contain a substance called fluoride. This helps to harden the enamel and makes it less vulnerable to acid. Many countries have fluoride in their water supplies.

Going to the dentist

Dirty tooth

The dentist scrapes off tartar which a toothbrush cannot remove.

Enamel

Tartar and plaque.

Fillings can be matched to the colour of your tooth.

Tooth after scraping and polishing.

You should have your teeth checked by a dentist at least twice a year so that problems can be treated before they get serious.

Dentists scrape tartar and plaque off your teeth and polish them. They remove decay by drilling away the bad area and filling the hole with a substance that hardens. This prevents the decay spreading. They can put new tops, or crowns, on badly damaged teeth, matching them to the others.

Taking care of your eyes

Your eyes work by picking up light rays reflected by objects around you. Cells lining the back of your eyes are sensitive to these rays and send the information they receive to your brain. On these two pages, you can find out more about this and how to keep your eyes healthy and shining.

How your eyes work

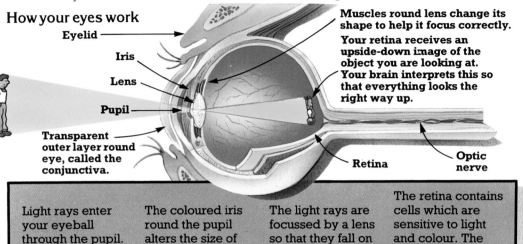

Eyelid

Iris

Lens

Pupil

Transparent outer layer round eye, called the conjunctiva.

Muscles round lens change its shape to help it focus correctly.

Your retina receives an upside-down image of the object you are looking at. Your brain interprets this so that everything looks the right way up.

Retina

Optic nerve

Light rays enter your eyeball through the pupil. This is the black hole in the centre of your eye.

The coloured iris round the pupil alters the size of the pupil to control the amount of light entering the eye.

The light rays are focussed by a lens so that they fall on to the retina which lines the back of the eye.

The retina contains cells which are sensitive to light and colour. The optic nerve sends messages from the retina to the brain.

Poor eyesight

Poor eyesight is usually caused by light rays not being focussed correctly on the retina. Things look blurred. This happens when the eyeball gets out of shape. It can be corrected by wearing glasses or contact lenses which bend the rays before they enter your eyes so they focus correctly on your retina (see below).

Testing your eyesight

If you cannot read a telephone directory with each eye at 49cm (19ins) or a car number plate at 23m (25yds), you should have your eyes checked as you may need glasses.

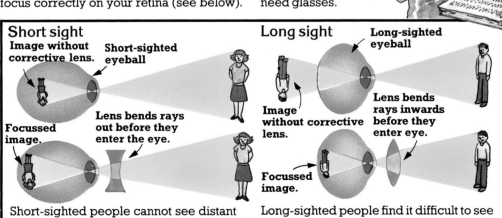

Short sight

Image without corrective lens.

Short-sighted eyeball

Focussed image.

Lens bends rays out before they enter the eye.

Short-sighted people cannot see distant objects clearly. The eyeball is too long and distant images are focussed before they reach the retina.

Long sight

Long-sighted eyeball

Image without corrective lens.

Lens bends rays inwards before they enter eye.

Focussed image.

Long-sighted people find it difficult to see close objects clearly. The eyeball is too short and images reach the retina before being focussed.

Choosing glasses

There are lots of different styles of glasses available. Light ones are less likely to give you headaches and rub your skin than heavy ones. They need to fit snugly so they do not slide down your nose.

Some glasses have shaded lenses. Others have lenses that react to different levels of light. They go dark in the sun to protect your eyes.

Contact lenses

Contact lenses may be easier to wear than glasses if you are very active. They float on the surface of your eye in front of the pupil. Soft contact lenses are more expensive and more comfortable but they need replacing about every two years.

Hard lenses last longer, although you need to replace them if your eyesight changes.

Dirt in your eyes

Tear gland, or lachrymal gland, above outside corner of eye.

Tears drain across eye into lachrymal sac.

Your eyes clean themselves naturally by producing tear fluid. This is why they water if you get dust in them. You can stimulate more tears by blowing your nose. If you get something in your eye you may be able to remove it by gently pulling the upper lid over the lower lid.

Never stick anything in your eye as you may damage it. If you cannot remove something from your eye, go to your local hospital casualty department.

Tired eyes

Looking into the blackness of your cupped hands relaxes the irises and the muscles round the lenses of your eyes.

If you do too much close work, especially in dim light, you may strain your eyes. Your eye muscles ache and you may get a headache. You may not blink enough so your eyes feel dry and sore.

Blinking a few times washes your eyes with tears and helps relieve soreness. Focussing on a distant object and gently rolling your eyes helps to relieve aching muscles. Cupping your hands over open eyes for a few minutes helps to rest them.

Bloodshot eyes

Camomile

Camomile tea bag.

If you are tired or have been outside in windy weather, your eyes may look bloodshot. This is caused by a dilation of blood capillaries in the conjunctiva.

You can relieve bloodshot eyes by soaking two camomile tea bags in cold water and placing one bag on each eye. The cold water and the camomile have a soothing, anti-inflammatory effect.

Eye infections

Conjunctivitis   **Blepharitis**   **Stye**

If your eyes are sticky, red, watery or painful, you may have an infection and should see your doctor. Conjunctivitis is an infection of the conjunctiva.

If the hair follicles of your eyelashes are inflamed making the eye look red-rimmed, it is called blepharitis.

The base of an eyelash may become infected and swell to form a stye. Do not use ointments on styes. Gently pressing cotton wool soaked in warm water against the stye may soothe it.

Caring for hands and feet

Your hands and feet are complex arrangements of lots of little bones. They get a lot of use, so it is worth looking after them. If your hands are sore or your feet hurt, life can be very uncomfortable.

Looking after your hands

If you put your hands in water a lot and do not dry them properly, they may get sore and scaly. Tap water is a very weak solution of chemicals but it is stronger than the moisture in your skin. Moisture moves out through the epidermis in an attempt to dilute the tap water. The process of water moving through a barrier to dilute a solution on the other side is called osmosis.

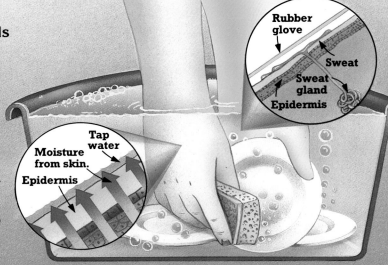

Wearing rubber gloves helps to protect your hands against water and detergents which dry out skin. If you wear gloves for longer than a few minutes, though, your hands will sweat a lot, which also dries them out. Hand cream helps prevent your hands from drying out or cracking in cold weather. You can also buy waterproof barrier creams to protect your hands when washing up and so on.

Nails

Like hair, nails are made up of dead cells growing from a living root, or matrix. This is underneath the cuticle at the base of the nail.

White spots on nails are caused by knocks to the matrix which damage new nail cells.

Keep cuticles supple by rubbing hand cream into them. Do not poke them with hard objects or you may hurt the matrix.

Bruised-looking nails may be caused by ill health, anaemia or smoking.

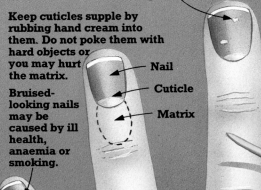

Nail
Cuticle
Matrix

Biting your nails

Biting nails weakens them and dirt from under them ends up in your mouth. You can buy bitter solutions to brush on your nails to help you stop biting them.

Cutting your nails

Cut your nails in an oval shape, level with the ends of your fingers. You may find it easier to do this using nail clippers or curved nail scissors.

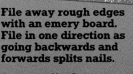

File away rough edges with an emery board. File in one direction as going backwards and forwards splits nails.

Remove dirt from under nails with the tip of an orange stick wrapped in cotton wool.

Looking after your feet

Your feet are made up of many bones, held in place by ligaments. It is easy to hurt your feet if you wear shoes which do not fit properly.

Buying shoes

Try shoes on and walk around before you buy them. Your feet swell up during the day and when it is hot, so take this into account when trying shoes on.

Shoes should fit snugly at your ankle so you do not have to bunch your toes up to keep them on.

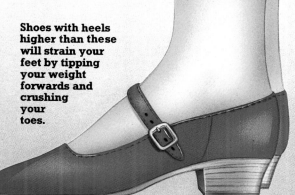

Shoes with heels higher than these will strain your feet by tipping your weight forwards and crushing your toes.

Shoes should be wide enough to let your toes lie naturally and not be squashed.

They should be about 1cm (1/3 in) longer than the foot to allow free movement.

Tired feet

Tired feet are often caused by ill-fitting shoes, high heels or non-stretch tights. Your ankles may swell if you are on your feet all day, especially in hot weather.

You can reduce swelling and rest your feet by lying down with your feet raised on cushions.

Flat feet

If the muscles forming the arch of your foot are weak, you may get flat feet. They may be strained by carrying your weight. These exercises should help:

1. With feet together, slowly rise up on tiptoes and down again. Repeat five times.

2. Put a pencil on the floor, place your toes over it and try to pick it up. Do this several times with each foot.

3. Walking barefoot is a good all-round exercise for feet.

Bunions

If you wear shoes that are too tight your big toe is bent sideways against your other toes. The joint may become inflamed and form a swelling called a bunion. If it becomes very painful this can be removed by surgery.

Athlete's Foot

If your skin is sore and peels in between your toes you may have an infection called Athlete's Foot. This is a fungus which grows on warm, damp feet. You can buy special creams or powders at a chemist to get rid of it.

Chilblains

In very cold weather, you may get painful, itchy patches on your toes, ankles, legs or hands. This is the result of blood vessels contracting excessively in the cold, cutting off the blood supply to parts of the tissue, which damages it. When you warm up, the damaged tissue hurts. Keep these parts warm with extra clothing. You can buy creams to help relieve chilblains.

Ingrown toenails

An ingrown toenail is a toenail that has curved over at the sides and grown into the flesh. This may happen naturally or it may be caused by tight shoes or socks. To prevent ingrown toenails, do not cut your nails too short or cut them away at the sides.

Cut toenails straight across. Do not try to shape them at the sides.

Looking after your back

Many people suffer from backache and related aches and pains. You can avoid some of these by taking care that you do not strain your back by standing and sitting or lifting and carrying things in the wrong way. Below you can see how your back works and how to avoid straining it.

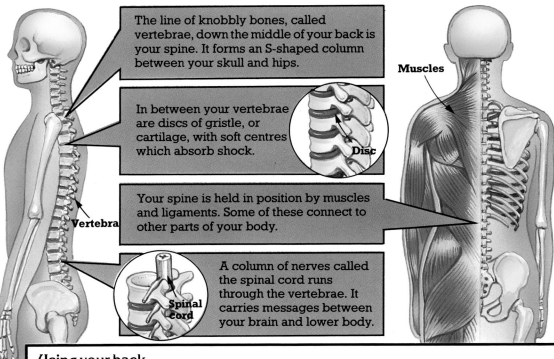

The line of knobbly bones, called vertebrae, down the middle of your back is your spine. It forms an S-shaped column between your skull and hips.

In between your vertebrae are discs of gristle, or cartilage, with soft centres which absorb shock.

Disc

Muscles

Your spine is held in position by muscles and ligaments. Some of these connect to other parts of your body.

Vertebra

A column of nerves called the spinal cord runs through the vertebrae. It carries messages between your brain and lower body.

Spinal cord

Using your back

Good posture means holding your body in a balanced way. This prevents you putting uneven pressure on your muscles and straining them.

Standing

Wrong   Right

Sitting

Wrong   Right

Sleeping

Soft mattress

Firm mattress

Stand up straight without leaning to one side. Keep your head up and relax your shoulders and back. Tuck your bottom in slightly. Imagine a straight line between your ear lobe, shoulder, knee and the front of your ankle.

The best seat height for your back allows your feet to rest on the floor with your thighs parallel to the floor. This avoids straining your lower back. A firm back rest helps. Do not cross your legs as this uses your back unevenly.

On a soft mattress, some of your back muscles have to work harder than others to support your spine. You can put planks under your mattress to make it firmer. Use enough pillows so that your head is supported in line with your spine.

Back strains

It is easy to damage the muscles, ligaments or tendons surrounding the spine by moving or twisting in an awkward way. This kind of strain usually heals itself in time but can be painful. You can soothe it by keeping the muscles warm with hot water bottles or baths. Always see your doctor if it is very bad.

Disc trouble

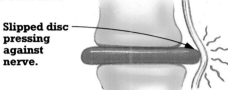

Slipped disc pressing against nerve.

If you continually hold your back in the wrong way and put pressure on it, you may cause one of your discs to slip out of position. This is called a slipped disc. If the damaged disc presses against a spinal nerve it can cause a lot of pain.

Slipped discs can be treated with rest, massage, heat treatment or one of the treatments described on the right. You can wear special supportive corsets. A board under your mattress will support your spine while you sleep.

Alexander Technique

The Alexander Technique is a way of improving posture. It is named after the doctor who invented it. He believed that bad posture causes all kinds of physical problems, including bad backs. The treatment involves massage, exercise and learning how to sit, stand and move properly.

Osteopathy and chiropractic

Osteopathy and chiropractic are ways of treating physical disorders by forms of massage and manipulation. The treatments are often used for back problems, though osteopaths and chiropractors believe that other illnesses can also be treated by working on the spine.

Exercise
Exercise such as yoga, swimming, walking and stretching all strengthen your back and help your posture.

Bending	Carrying	Shifting heavier weights

Wrong **Right**

Hold single weights close in front of you.

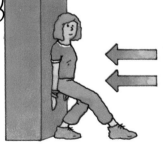

When lifting things, bend your legs and keep your back as straight as possible. This is because your leg muscles are stronger than your back muscles. Kneel to do things such as cleaning the bath instead of bending over.

When carrying a weight such as a typewriter or a baby, hold it close in front of you. Rather than carrying one bag of shopping, carry two smaller ones, one in each hand. This prevents the spine from being pulled sideways.

The safest way to shift a heavy weight is to lean your back against it and push. When pushing things such as a lawn mower, put your whole body into it. Try to move heavy furniture by rocking it rather than lifting it.

Rest and relaxation

Rest and relaxation are just as important to your body as exercise and healthy eating. If you do not get enough of them you can make yourself ill. Your body is a bit like a battery. If it is not allowed to recharge itself through sleep and relaxation it may stop working properly.

Why you need sleep

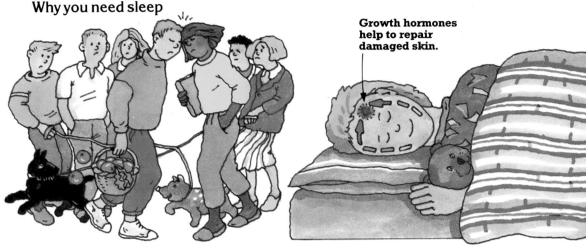

Growth hormones help to repair damaged skin.

Lack of sleep affects your ability to concentrate. When you dream, your brain may be clearing itself out and preparing itself for the next day's thinking.

During your teens, you need at least eight hours sleep a night. If you stay out late, try to go to bed early the next night. The effects of lack of sleep can build up over several days.

When you are awake you make many demands on your mind and body. Your body needs a period of rest to repair itself and prevent itself from getting worn out. During sleep, substances called hormones stimulate body tissues to grow and repair themselves.

Children need more sleep than adults because there is more growing to do.

Preparing for a better sleep
If you have trouble getting to sleep, or want a really good night's sleep, try the following things.

Leave a window slightly open but make sure you are warm enough.

Try reading a book to calm your mind.

Take some exercise during the evening. This will help your muscles relax.

Avoid tea, coffee, or food before bedtime. A hot, milky drink may help you relax, though.

What causes stress?

When you feel anger, fear or anxiety your body produces hormones such as adrenalin and noradrenalin to gear it up for action. They prepare your body for fighting or running away.

If you are continually anxious, your body goes through this reaction over and over again. This can cause stress. If you do not carry out the physical responses for which your body is prepared, the hormones build up. This leads to tension and tiredness.

Stress can lower your resistance to illness and lead to headaches, indigestion and sleeplessness. It may in time lead to more serious complaints such as asthma, stomach ulcers, high blood pressure and heart disease.

Your heart beats faster and your blood pressure rises.

Extra blood is directed to muscle groups for running or fighting.

Your temperature rises and you sweat more to control it.

More sugar is released into the blood for energy.

Your breathing becomes deeper and faster to take in more oxygen.

— QUIET —
EXAM IN
PROGRESS

How to avoid stress

Try to work out the causes of your anxiety. Discuss it with someone and try to find a way of avoiding it or changing your attitude to it. Set aside part of each day for relaxation.

Relaxation

| Lie on the floor or on your bed. | Tense your toes as tightly as you can, then slowly relax them. | Carry on slowly tensing and relaxing all the different muscle groups in your body, travelling up your legs and the rest of your body. |

If you are anxious, your body may be tense even if you are not aware of it. This can be exhausting. The exercise above might help you to relax.

Deep breathing

If you are upset you may breathe in short sharp pants, using only the top half of your rib cage. To calm down, breathe deeply and slowly several times, making your chest rise and fall. Breathing like this can help you calm down before a stressful experience such as an interview.

Meditation

If your mind is buzzing with worries you may feel tired but be unable to relax. You can relax your mind by concentrating on something soothing. This is known as meditation. You can learn the techniques in special classes and it is also used in Yoga. Here is a meditation exercise. Keep at it for at least ten minutes.

Sit comfortably, close your eyes and try to relax. Breathe regularly. Think of a soothing scene, such as a peaceful lake and concentrate on it. Try to blot out other thoughts.

Massage

If you are under stress, your neck and shoulder muscles tend to tense up which may give you headaches. Massaging them will help you relax them. Here is a simple massage you can do with a friend.

1. Sit your friend down and stand behind him or her.

2. Place hands on shoulders, thumbs reaching down back.

3. Gently squeeze muscles and flesh without pinching.

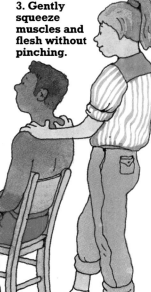

Smoking, alcohol and drugs

Advertisements may make you think that alcoholic drinks or cigarettes will make you feel good. Although they may be pleasant at first, they can be bad for you in the long term and they can become addictive (very difficult to give up). Here you can find out about the effects cigarettes and alcohol can have on your body and also about what other drugs, such as pot, do to you.

What smoking does to you

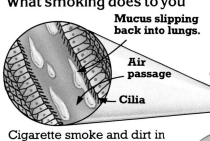

Mucus slipping back into lungs.

Air passage

Cilia

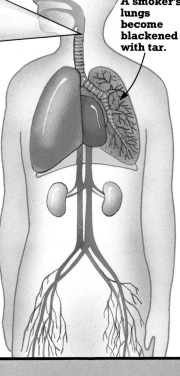

A smoker's lungs become blackened with tar.

Cigarette smoke and dirt in the air stimulate the cells lining your air passages to produce more mucus, or phlegm.

The mucus traps any dirt and it is pushed back up your air passages by little hairs, called cilia. By blowing your nose or spitting it out you keep your lungs clear.

When you inhale cigarette smoke, your cilia stop working. Mucus carrying waste substances, tar and nicotine slips back down into your lungs. Eventually the cilia stop working even when you are not smoking.

Lung cancer
Certain cells in your lungs fight bacteria by engulfing them. They also engulf tar from smoke. Chemicals in the tar can start lung cells changing into cancer cells which multiply, destroy the lungs and spread around the body to start new cancers.

Chronic bronchitis
Tar and mucus may damage the small air tubes and air sacs in your lungs. This can lead to dangerous diseases such as chronic bronchitis. This makes you pant when taking even gentle exercise.

Heart disease
Carbon dioxide and other gases in cigarette smoke increase your pulse rate and blood pressure. This may cause fatty deposits to build up in your arteries, leading to severe heart disease.

Reasons not to smoke
Here are some reasons why you should not start smoking.

★ Most people do not smoke because they do not want to risk their lives. They also prefer not to have to put up with other people's smoke.

★ Cigarette smoke makes your clothes, hair and breath stink.

★ It is unpleasant for non-smokers to kiss or come into close contact with smokers.

If you decide to stop smoking, here are some things which might help.

★ Take up a new sport or fitness activity. The fitter you become, the less you will want to damage your lungs with cigarettes.

★ For a couple of months, put the money you would otherwise spend on cigarettes in a jar. Then buy yourself a treat with it at the end.

★ Tell your friends you have given up and ask them not to offer you cigarettes.

What does alcohol do to you?

Alcohol is in drinks such as beer, wine and spirits. A couple of drinks cannot harm you but alcohol can easily become addictive. Below you can read about what happens to alcohol in your body.

Alcohol taken to brain while waiting to enter liver.

Your liver can only absorb 28gm (1/3 oz) of alcohol per hour.

This equals:
1/3 glass of beer.
or
1/9 bottle of wine.
or
7/10 measure of spirits.

Alcohol is a mild poison. If you drink more than a small amount it is pumped round your body in your blood while it waits to be absorbed and neutralized by your liver.

When it reaches your brain, it affects your speech, actions, senses and judgement. This is why it is very dangerous to drive if you have been drinking. Too much alcohol causes headaches, sickness and thirst the next day. This is called a hangover.

Why drinking can be dangerous

Healthy liver

Liver after years of heavy drinking.

If you drink heavily, your liver has to continually overwork to digest the alcohol and make you sober. This may lead to liver damage, including fatal diseases such as cirrhosis of the liver.

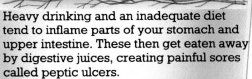

Part of stomach eaten away by digestive juices.

Heavy drinking and an inadequate diet tend to inflame parts of your stomach and upper intestine. These then get eaten away by digestive juices, creating painful sores called peptic ulcers.

Too much alcohol can also damage your brain and weaken your heart muscles.

Being addicted to alcohol is a disease known as alcoholism. It can be cured and you should seek help from your doctor if you or anyone you know is an addict.

How other drugs affect you

There are a number of other drugs which you may be tempted to try. People may tell you stories about the wonderful feelings that they give you. However they cause your body enormous harm; thousands of people die from drug abuse every year. Below you can find out about some of the most common drugs.

Drug and description	Danger
Marijuana. Known as pot or hash. Usually smoked.	Similar dangers to tobacco, as it irritates your lungs. Can create malformed sperm and harm unborn babies.
Spirit-based glue. Usually sniffed.	Contains complex chemicals which can destroy your nasal tissue and damage your lungs.
Cocaine. Fine white powder derived from cocoa shrub. Usually sniffed.	This drug can damage your lungs for life. Highly addictive and very expensive.
LSD. Usually taken in white pills.	LSD puts you in a strange, sometimes terrifying world. This is called a "trip". It can cause permanent brain damage.
Heroin. Greyish-brown powder from the juice of the poppy flower, or artificially made.	One of the most addictive and poisonous of all drugs. Your body quickly gets used to a high level and needs more. Heroin addicts suffer pain and become desperate if they cannot get enough.
Tranquillizers, stimulants and sleeping pills.	Some people find these drugs addictive if they take them for too long.

Growing up

Between the ages of about 10 and 18 you go through many physical and emotional changes. This time, called puberty, is the stage between being a child and being an adult.

During puberty, your body starts to produce more hormones which stimulate your body to change. The pictures show some of these changes and how to deal with them.

What happens to boys?

Your voice box, or larynx, grows bigger, making your voice break. While this is happening, your voice might sound husky or alternate between being squeaky and deep.

You grow hair and new sweat glands under your arms and around your penis. Sweat starts to smell sour after a few hours. You may get used to the smell yourself but others will notice it. Make sure you wash these areas once a day. You can use a deodorant under your arms as well to prevent the smell of stale sweat.

Over the years you develop more muscle. The exercises and activities shown earlier in the book, especially on pages 8-9, 14-15 and 20-21 will help you build muscle.

Different parts of your body grow at different rates. Your limbs might grow very fast and you might get taller before you get broader. You may feel gangly and awkward for a while.

You grow hair on your face and eventually need to start shaving. You can probably get rid of hair fastest using an electric razor. However, foam, warm water and a non-electric razor may give you a closer shave.

Your chest and shoulders get broader as you develop a bigger heart and lungs. These changes happen slowly.

Some boys grow hair on their chests.

Your penis and testes get bigger. The left testis usually hangs down slightly lower than the right one.
   The testes start to produce sperm (male sex cells) and the male sex hormone, which is called testosterone. This hormone is responsible for many of the other changes that take place in your body during puberty.

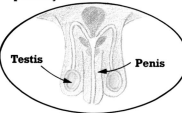

Testis   Penis

What happens to girls?

Hair grows under your arms and around your vagina. You can shave underarm hair if you like but many women do not.

More sweat glands develop in these areas so wash them once a day. You can wear a deodorant under your arms. (See the advice given for boys on the previous page.)

Inside your body, parts of you develop to enable you to have children. Your ovaries start to produce an egg each month. Unless it is fertilized by a sperm and you get pregnant, your body discharges the egg along with the womb's lining of blood. This is called your period and lasts a few days.

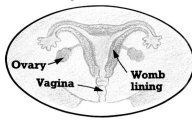

You can use a tampon or a sanitary towel to absorb your period blood. You need to change them two or three times a day. You can go swimming or do any exercise wearing a tampon. It cannot slip. Sanitary towels are absorbent pads which you wear between your legs.

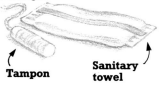

Tampon   **Sanitary towel**

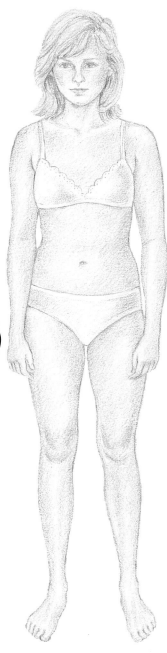

Your breasts begin to develop. Unless they are fairly small and light you may find it comfortable to wear a bra to support them. You may need a bra if you do a lot of jogging, for instance, because your breasts bounce around and get sore.

Everyone is a different shape so try several bras and find one that suits you before you buy one.

You cannot alter your breast size by exercising as breasts contain no muscles. However, exercise such as swimming can strengthen surrounding muscles and help them support your breasts.

Your hips get wider so that they will be broad enough to carry a baby and give birth.

Some women get pains in the lower stomach and back before or during a period. You can buy painkillers for this. It is caused by the womb contracting to push out the blood. Gentle activity may help, such as swimming or walking.

You may also feel particularly moody, depressed or tearful before a period. Be patient with yourself and the moods will pass. If any of these problems gets really bad, see a doctor.

93

Checking your fitness progress

Below is a chart of sports and activities which will improve your stamina, strength and suppleness. If you want to develop any of these aspects, concentrate on a selection of the activities listed under the relevant heading. Activities which are especially good for a particular aspect of fitness are shown in bold type. Those which appear under more than one heading are good for improving more than one aspect.

STAMINA	STRENGTH	SUPPLENESS
badminton	badminton	badminton
basketball	**boxing**	**dancing**
boxing	**canoeing**	**fencing**
cycling	fencing	football (rugby and soccer)
dancing	football (rugby and soccer)	cricket
football (rugby and soccer)	gymnastics	gymnastics
gymnastics	hockey	judo
brisk walking	horse-riding	netball
hockey	judo	rock-climbing
jogging	netball	sailing
netball	**rowing**	skating (roller and ice)
rowing	running	skiing (cross-country)
running	sailing	**squash**
skating (roller and ice)	skating (roller and ice)	**swimming**
skiing (cross-country)	**skiing (cross-country)**	table-tennis
skipping	squash	tennis
squash	**swimming**	**yoga**
swimming	tennis	
tennis	**weight-training**	
wind-surfing	wind-surfing	

Measuring your progress

Here are some ideas for how to monitor your improvement as you get fitter.

Strength   Keep a record of how many press-ups or other muscle-building exercises you can do. Try to push yourself a bit further each week.

Suppleness   Stand in front of a mirror as you do your suppleness exercises. As you find you can stretch further, you will be able to see a difference.

Stamina   Copy the chart below, adding extra lines of boxes for as many weeks as you like. Each time you take some stamina-building exercise, write it in on the chart. Take your pulse before and after the exercise and fill in the time for which you exercised. Aim to get your pulse rate after exercise to within the target training zone (see page 57). As you get fitter, your pulse rate after exercise may drop. You will have to do more to keep it within the target training zone.

The chart has been filled in to show you how to do it but the pulse rates are only examples. Yours may be different.

	Activity	Time spent exercising	Pulse before activity	Pulse after activity
Week 1	SWIMMING DANCING BADMINTON	15 MINUTES 1½ HOURS 1 HOUR	72 68 75	125 119 105
Week 2				

Index

First published in 1986 by Usborne Publishing Ltd., Usborne House, 83-85 Saffron Hill, London EC1N 8RT, England.

© Usborne Publishing 1991, 1986

The name Usborne and the device ⬤ are Trade Marks of Usborne Publishing Ltd.

Printed in Belgium